A Jon Stanton Thriller by

VICTOR METHOS

122

It's so much darker when a light goes out than it would have been if it had never shone.

—John Steinbeck

1

Jon Stanton sat down on the bench and pressed his elbow against the Desert Eagle in the holster on his hip under his leather jacket. The reassurance of the gun calmed him as he stared into the gray eyes across from him. The man wore a biker's jacket, his white, greasy hair coming down over his eyes. He lifted a cigarette and blew smoke in Stanton's face.

"Money first," the man said, his voice gravelly from a lifetime of smoking.

Stanton lifted the gym bag by his feet and set it on the table between them. As he reached for the zipper, the man grabbed his hand and said, "I'll look."

Stanton slowly withdrew his hand, holding the man's gaze. He unzipped the bag and checked the rubber-banded wads of hundred-dollar bills that filled the bag. He zipped it up again with a smile.

"You're not going to count it?" Stanton said.

"No need. If it ain't all here, I'm gonna find ya and kill ya."

The man lifted the bag and motioned with his head for Stanton to follow him. At the park around the corner, three of his biker buddies were smoking a joint near their bikes, the sun glistening off their

7

sweating foreheads. Honolulu had reached a record high of 101 degrees the day before and felt only slightly cooler that day, yet the bikers still wore their jackets.

Behind the bikes, a white van parked in the stall nearest the exit. A man with a scraggly beard sat in the driver's seat with a woman beside him. Neither of them paid any attention as Stanton was led to the back, and the man dropped the gym bag to open the doors to the van.

Inside, three young girls squinted in the sudden light. Wearing only a hint of lingerie to cover themselves, they were dirty and bound together with rope. Stanton had to look away.

"That bitch there, she like sixteen, fresh off the boat, brother. Taiwan or China or somethin'. She tight as shit. But that one, she like thirteen and she fights like a muthafucker. You gonna have to beat her down some. But she'll get used to the cock after a while." He spit on the concrete. "So Todd said you gonna sell 'em. If you want more, we can get 'em. Got the hookup back east, brother."

Stanton closed his eyes a moment. A breeze blew his hair softly and tickled his forehead. One word and this would be over. Twelve officers surrounding the parking lot would rush in. But then all of the bikers would surrender. This man who stood in front of him had kidnapped, raped, and sold hundreds of girls over the years. The youngest they'd found was four years old, an orphan from a province in China where half the population died of disease or starvation. The humanitarian volunteers who found her decided selling her sounded better than shipping her to an orphanage in one of the big cities. And that girl, who could barely speak, led them to this man: Randall Hersh, known as Switch in one of the most brutal biker gangs on the islands.

"How many more can you get?" Stanton said.

Randall grinned. "Many as you need. You can try 'em, too. Have a taste before buying. I ain't got no problem with that. Just gotta wear a rubber so you don't knock 'em up. Abortion's, like, eight hundred bucks."

Stanton pressed his elbow to his gun again. If he gave the word, there wouldn't be a fight. There would be arrests, lawyers, court appearances, sentences, prison time, and a release date, when he could walk back out into the sunshine to do it again.

Slowly, almost imperceptibly, Stanton pulled back his jacket. Just enough so that Randall could see the gleaming steel of his weapon. And then Stanton closed the jacket again.

"Let's put in another order," Stanton said.

Randall glanced at his buddies. "Sure. Hop in and we'll talk."

"In the van?"

"Yeah, man. Away from prying eyes and all that shit."

Neither blinked nor spoke. In his peripheral vision Stanton could see Randall's three buddies lining up behind him.

"Something wrong?" Stanton said.

"Nah, brother. Just need to work a few things out."

"Yeah, and what's that?"

Randall smiled and turned as though he were looking at the girls. At the last moment he spun around, whipping out a Beretta. Stanton grabbed his forearm, aiming the pistol away from him. A shot went off. The three bikers rushed in from behind.

Stanton twisted around, his back pressed against Randall, the biker's Beretta still in its owner's hand, which was now caught under

Stanton's arm. He squeezed the trigger. A round drilled into one of the bikers' chests and knocked him back. Stanton fired twice more. The other two, still standing, pulled out their weapons and Stanton spun back and held Randall in front of him, forcing the man's gun up under his own chin.

"Easy, brother," Randall said, his free hand coming up in surrender. "Just friends here. Just talkin'."

The cars screeched to a stop across the parking lot, detectives and uniformed officers with Kevlar vests jumping out. Stanton loosened his grip on Randall, but he didn't move. He didn't attack, and he didn't try to get away. Stanton let him go.

The officers screamed for everyone to get on the ground. One of them called in emergency services for the man Stanton had shot. The others overwhelmed the other three men, throwing them to the ground, slapping cuffs on them, and hauling them away as they spit and swore. A police truck pulled up, and the officers piled the men and the one woman inside.

Kai, Stanton's captain, sauntered over—three hundred pounds of surly Hawaiian. "You okay?"

"Fine. Thanks."

Kai looked back at the police truck. "You gettin' too old for this, hoaloha. We got younger detectives."

Stanton put his hands on his hips. Sweat dripped down into his eyes, and he let it sting. "I'm good."

"You sure?"

Stanton nodded. "I want to know who they're getting their girls from."

Kai shrugged. Stanton knew this bust was all Kai had wanted: some media attention, a homicide off the board—a young woman Randall had sold to a man who beat her to death—and a few of the biker gang behind bars. But that wasn't enough for Stanton. He was tired of working on the peripheries, throwing resources at the problem and never getting to the core. Not ever.

Kai looked into the truck. "Shit, hoaloha, maybe sometimes it's better not knowin' how everything is, ya know?"

2

The police precinct in Honolulu's first district looked more like an office building than police headquarters. Stanton parked his Jeep at the curb. Across the street sat the only palace still standing in the United States, which had belonged to the last queen of Hawaii. There were two stories of what had happened: either she sold Hawaii to the United States and Britain, or she was forced out of power and the islands conquered. Stanton could believe either, and it wouldn't have surprised him.

He took the elevator to the fifth floor, the detectives' floor, or what the precinct called "the detectives' table." Unlike most major police agencies, although Honolulu PD did have specializations, detectives were expected to cross into other fields. A Homicide detective might have to deal with a property crime and a Missing Persons detective might have to investigate money laundering. For the most part, Stanton had been left alone to work homicides. He and Kai went back a long way, and Kai knew what Stanton specialized in: the cases no one else wanted.

Stanton sat down in the bull pen and logged on to his computer. He'd have to get a psychiatric evaluation because of the shooting, but Honolulu didn't have mandatory leave after an officer involved shooting like San Diego PD had. He only needed a clearance from IAD, which he'd gotten within three hours, and Stanton could get back to work the same day.

The browser opened to an article in the *Journal of Forensic Psychiatry* on necrophilia, profiling a woman who could reach sexual climax only after bathing her lovers in ice during intercourse to mimic a corpse. Stanton had seen the phenomenon before.

"That looks interesting," his partner, Laka, said. She pulled her hair back with an elastic band and leaned down, reading a few lines over his shoulder. "Have you ever tried just checking Twitter or reading a gossip blog or something?"

He grinned. "Only if they talk about necrophilia."

She slapped his shoulder. "You're so weird." She straightened up. "Your collar's here. He's in three."

Stanton closed the article and rose. Though interrogation room five, farthest away from everything, was Stanton's favorite, three was the only one with a window looking outside the building. He found it distracting during an interview, but the blue skies helped to counteract the horror he sometimes heard spewing from the mouths of men in that room.

Randall Hersh sat handcuffed at the gray table. Stanton shut the door and sat down across from him. He glanced at the red light on the camera in the corner, indicating it was on.

"Your friend is gonna live. I missed his heart by two inches."

Randall shrugged. "Whatever."

"You don't care."

"He wasn't patched yet. Didn't have his colors. He wasn't a Black Sun."

Stanton glanced out the window at a plane leaving a white contrail as it streaked across the sky. "I want to know where you get your girls from."

"I bet you do. But that ain't gonna happen. See, this ain't my first go 'round. You gonna call my lawyer and press charges then he's gonna get me a short sentence. Maybe three years. Maybe two when the prosecutor realizes how much money the Suns donate to his reelection campaign every four years."

Stanton smirked. "Donating to campaigns? You don't sound like any biker I've talked to, Randall."

"Different world. Them days of ridin' 'round shootin' at cops is over. There're better ways to get things done."

Stanton rubbed the bridge of his nose and sighed audibly. A coming migraine thumped inside his head, and he wished he'd had a Diet Coke and some Advil before going in. "Just between me and you, why didn't you run or fight back? I gave you a chance."

Randall chuckled. "'Cause I ain't some punk outta high school. I been doin' this a long time. Met a lotta cops. And I know when a cop wants me to give him an excuse. You was hopin' I'd run so you could pop me. And I didn't feel like dyin' yet today."

"I didn't kill your friend."

"You was firing with me holding the gun and you only missed by two inches. You meant to kill him, too." He leaned back in his seat. "Nah, I know when you fight and when you give in. I ain't goin' up against some maniac cop just to die."

Stanton bit down, flexing his jaw muscles. He left the room silently and shut the door behind him. Laka stood in the observation room, watching Randall through the one-way glass.

"What d'ya wanna do?" she asked.

"Get him his lawyer."

3

By four p.m., Stanton had left the precinct and headed to his psychiatrist's office for his biweekly session. Despite his own PhD in psychology, Stanton had been in therapy off and on since the age of ten. His father, himself a psychiatrist, believed therapy was as much a necessary part of living in modern society as having a Social Security number and a place to live.

Dr. Natalia Vaquer was standing in front of her receptionist when Stanton walked in. She wore a brown suit with glasses that made her look like a professor or librarian. Dr. Vaquer smiled. "You're early, Jon. But as it happens, my last appointment cancelled."

"Yeah, sorry. I come early sometimes. I just like the quiet."

She stepped over to the double doors leading into her office and opened them. Every time he went through those doors, he felt transported to another world in which he could be totally and completely honest. He had never had that relationship with anyone before. Not his wife, not the fiancée he'd lost, not previous therapists, no one… except for maybe one man: Eli Sherman, a partner convicted of killing two women and later escaping police custody. The last Stanton had heard, he had disappeared somewhere in South America.

"You look good, Jon," she said, sitting down in her leather chair. "I meant to tell you last time."

"Thanks," he said, settling into the couch. "I've lost about twelve pounds. Started jogging again. I think it calms me… maybe gets some of my nervous energy out."

"I often recommend exercise to my patients. It permanently boosts endorphin and norepinephrine levels in the brain. It makes you a happier person." She paused. "How's the Prozac?"

"It's fine. I think we're at a good dosage. Not enough to have any real side effects."

"It's not supposed to have *any* side effects."

Stanton shook his head. "There've been some instances of psychotic breaks in younger patients taking fluoxetine long term—schoolyard shootings, murdering parents, suicide, sadism. I sometimes think the mind is too complex to fully predict what a substance will and won't do to us. Anyway, the insomnia's more of a problem now."

"When you do sleep, do you dream?"

"Sometimes."

"What do you dream about?"

Stanton looked over at her desk. On the edge was a statue of a dancing man in a mask—African, maybe Maasai. "That's new," he said.

"My husband brought it from Kenya. He's a photographer. But I'd like to stay on point. What do you dream about?"

He swallowed. "Same as everyone else. Sex, memories from childhood, work…" He hesitated. "My sister."

She leaned forward. "I know we've talked about this before, but the last time we spoke of your sister, you were considering flying back up to Seattle to see if you could find out how she went missing and what happened to her. And then you never went. Why?"

"They, ah… they found a house in a suburb up there. Belonged to a schoolteacher who'd passed away and didn't have a family, so the heirs sold the house. The new owners decided to gut the house and remodel before reselling it. Under the floorboards in the basement, they found a body wrapped in a garbage bag. The police were called out, and they tore up the entire house and the backyard. They found sixteen bodies total, all young girls." He paused. "The teacher taught at my sister's high school."

Dr. Vaquer held his gaze. "Was one of the bodies her?"

He shook his head. "I don't know. I read about the story online. Never followed up."

"Why not?"

He shrugged.

"Jon, your sister's disappearance even according to you is the most important event in your childhood, the thing everything else is connected to. Probably the reason you became a police officer, why you have trouble in committed relationships… everything ties back. And you're telling me you have an opportunity to find out what happened, and you didn't follow up on it?"

"I can't… I'm not sure I could handle knowing what happened, knowing what she went through."

"I'm sure whatever you're imagining happened is probably worse. In my experience, knowing the truth is cathartic. No matter how painful that truth is."

He hesitated. "There's something else, too. Today, I busted a human trafficker. Just some low-life, the same type I've busted dozens of times. We had a homicide of a woman who was killed by a man who claimed he had bought her from someone else. And then Juvenile Crimes found a four-year-old girl who gave us the location and physical description of the man who'd kidnapped her and forced…"

He stopped. Sometimes he forgot that other people, even psychiatrists, weren't accustomed to seeing and hearing what he saw and heard every day. Frequently Stanton shocked other people who only casually asked him how work was or what he had done that day. He had learned not to discuss it unless necessary.

"She'd been forced to do things, and she had a fantastic memory. Smart little girl. She described where it happened, and the detectives recognized the location. So we tracked this man down. I volunteered to fake a purchase. Three young women, that was the deal, and today was the day. I was supposed to signal the other detectives when we had the evidence and the girls were safe. But I didn't do it. I didn't give them the signal."

"Why not?"

"I… I wanted them to fight. I even let him go. He'd tried to shoot me, and I let him go, hoping he'd try it again so I could put a bullet in his head. I shot one of his buddies, too. I tried to kill him but missed. He survived."

She didn't say anything for a moment. "Jon, that's very serious, what you just told me. I'm concerned."

He nodded slowly. "Yeah, I'm concerned, too."

4

After the session, Stanton drove home. He lived near the North Shore not far from the beach in a house he'd bought when he was making piles of money as a private investigator, and his fiancée was making just as much as a consultant. Now it seemed too big for one man: six bedrooms, a balcony, a basement… All he ever used were the living room, the kitchen, and his bedroom. As he walked in, he wondered if it was time to sell. The only thing stopping him was the proximity to the ocean. He could see it from the patio or the balcony, and at night he could hear the surf rolling in to shore. When he left the balcony doors open upstairs, it lulled him to sleep.

Stanton left his gun on the dining room table with his wallet. He stepped onto the patio and stared at the crystal blue water. Before moving to Hawaii, he'd seen images online of beaches where the water was so blue it looked like melted gems. He thought at the time that the photo had simply caught the water at the most opportune time, and then someone had doctored the photo a little. But when he got here, he saw that the photos were accurate. There were beaches where the water was completely transparent. Looking down from a boat, he could see to the bottom. The beach near him reflected the sun in a vibrant sapphire. He sat down and watched the waves foam as he called his sons. Mathew was now at Boston College studying anthropology, and his younger son, Jon Junior, was still in high school. He tried both their cell phones, but neither one answered, so he left messages.

As he was going back in, his cell phone buzzed. The ID said "Laka."

"Hey," he answered.

"Hey, I'm sorry to bug you. I know you're at home."

"No worries. What's up?"

"I have a pretty bad domestic violence and was wondering if you could back me up. I got some uniforms here but I wanted you to have first crack at the husband. You're better at that than I am."

"Better at what?"

"I don't know. Just getting people to talk, I guess."

"I'll come down, but that's not true. You're a good detective, Laka."

"Thanks. I'll text you the address."

Stanton was out the door in a few minutes, stopping again briefly on the patio to watch the ocean. Laka had been a detective a little over a year and still had problems soliciting information. She took a stance of division: us and them. Stanton didn't see it that way. Anyone was capable of anything.

He'd seen a lot of good people, people in positions of trust and power, turn to bad people in a moment. Sometimes it was gradual, but sometimes the transformation was instant. One moment everyone knew who the person was, and the next the person was someone else that no one ever would've imagined they could become.

The address was on a street he knew well: Haluka Drive. The government-subsidized housing was the one place on the island other than Chinatown that the police didn't like going at night.

Several cruisers and an ambulance were already at the address by the time Stanton pulled up. The lawn in front of the brown house was missing patches of grass. He hopped out of his Jeep and pushed his sunglasses up on his head. The pit bull chained up in the front seemed too skinny and lethargic, its brown fur with black stripes stretched tight over visible ribs and a head that seemed far too big for its body. Stanton leaned down. The dog looked up at him lazily. He reached through the fence and ran his finger over the dog's snout. The dog closed its eyes as though appreciating the contact with another living creature.

Inside the house, a local islander sat on the couch with his wrists cuffed behind him, a uniformed officer next to him. The odor of alcohol was overwhelming. Near the back door, Laka stood with a crying woman. The woman had a swollen eye, and EMTs were looking at some injuries to her arms. Laka noticed him, said something to the woman, and came over.

"Jon, this is Mr. Akina. He goes by Robert."

Stanton sat down next to the man. "The cuffs aren't necessary, Officer."

The uniform hesitated a moment and then uncuffed the man.

"Thank you," Robert said.

"My name is Jon." He glanced at the woman. "She your wife?" Robert nodded. "I was married once," Stanton said.

Robert chuckled softly. "Ain't easy, man. They don't tell you nothin' when you gettin' into it."

"No, they don't. Like that you're going to give up some of the things you love most."

"Yeah. I had me a Harley, man. Softail."

Stanton whistled through his teeth. "That's a nice bike."

He nodded. "Spent my savings on it." He looked at his wife. "She made me sell it. Said there was no reason for it. No fucking reason. I used to love goin' around the island, man. Wind over my face, you know?"

"Yeah. Freedom."

"Yeah, man. Freedom. *Me ka aloha.* Just out by myself. I ain't got no time for myself no more."

Stanton hesitated. "I know you love her, Robert. And I know you're sorry. But your natural defenses are coming up right now. You're hurt that you would allow yourself to do something like this. And so you're trying to justify it, trying to come up with reasons she deserved it. That way you don't have to believe what you did was so horrible." Stanton placed his hand on the man's shoulder. "You don't have to do that. Don't hide from the truth—it doesn't solve anything." Stanton paused. "Trust me, I know."

Tears came to Robert's eyes. "I love her, man. I do. She just pisses me off so much sometimes I lose my shit."

"It's okay to lose your temper. Just don't let it devour you."

Stanton left his hand on Robert's shoulder while the man began his statement. Stanton pointedly glanced up at the officer, who said, "Oh," and fumbled with a notepad before hurriedly scribbling down notes as Robert spoke. It was a story Stanton had heard a thousand times: he got drunk, they got into a fight, he resorted to violence.

After telling the story, Robert was handcuffed again and taken to the cruiser.

"*Mahalo*," Robert said, thanking Stanton.

"*He me iki ia*," Stanton replied. *It's nothing.* He waited until Robert was in the cruiser before walking over to check on the victim.

The wife's face had swelled up so much that one of her eyes had completely closed. The EMTs said her left arm was fractured, and they wanted to take her down to the ER. She kept repeating, "I don't want to press charges."

Laka listened and explained softly why she needed to cooperate, that this would keep happening over and over. She had to make a clean break, and there were resources available to her. But the woman insisted that it was just a drunken mistake that wouldn't happen again.

When the woman and Laka had paused, both realizing the other wasn't about to give up, Stanton said, "I'm sorry about what happened. I have one question before I leave, though. That dog in the yard is malnourished. When was the last time it was fed?"

The woman looked at him as though he were crazy. "The dog? I don't know."

"Well, I'd like to go buy some dog food, but I need to make sure it's actually going to be used."

"Who gives a shit about a dog? You can take him and put him down if you want."

Stanton was silent a moment. "You want us to get rid of him?"

"I don't care. Do whatever you want. I don't want him no more."

Stanton turned away.

He left the house as Robert was driven away. He went over to the dog and unchained him. "Come on, buddy. Come on." An empty food bowl sat near the dog, with the name "Hanny" on it. Stanton wasn't sure if that actually was the dog's name, but he liked it.

"Come on, Hanny. Come on."

The dog didn't have the strength to move. He had just enough strength to rest his chin on Stanton's palm. Stanton sat down and let Hanny rest on his left thigh as he scratched behind his ears. Stanton felt the dog's heartbeat against his leg. It was slow—in addition to starving, the dog was dehydrated and sick.

Stanton slid his arms underneath the dog and picked him up, pressed him against his chest, and walked back to the Jeep.

5

The nearest veterinary clinic, almost all the way across the island, had an ER run by two veterinarians and their four assistants. Stanton had been there once before when his partner, Laka, had a cat that required surgery.

Stanton's vehicle was the only one in the lot. He carried Hanny inside and told the assistant at the front desk what had happened. She immediately led him into the back and laid the dog on a gurney. The veterinarian and another assistant began checking him, and Stanton left the room and went to sit in the lobby. Leaning his head against the wall, he took a deep breath and stared up at the ceiling. He'd been in similar situations before, but never at a vet clinic. Usually he'd be in some hospital corridor waiting for a victim to gather the courage to speak to him. Maybe he'd get a description of the attacker, maybe he wouldn't get anything. The darkness he'd seen over and over again came in different forms. Robert Akina had that darkness in him, though he considered himself a good man. Outwardly, other than beating his wife, he may have been. But it didn't matter. The darkness would take what it wanted. Stanton had no doubt that, one day, he'd be called out to Robert's house on a homicide rather than a domestic violence incident.

An hour passed before the vet came out. Hands in his pockets, he grinned and said, "He's gonna be okay, Detective. Really malnourished, and there's an infection on his hind leg. I'm putting him on antibiotics, and some rest and weight gain should get him back up to 100 percent. Um, did you want us to notify the shelter to come get him?"

Stanton rose. Over the vet's shoulder, he could see into the room. Hanny was sitting up and digging ferociously into a silver bowl of canned dog food. The assistant who had checked them in was cleaning and bandaging the wound on his hind leg.

"What happens at the shelter?" Stanton said.

"They'll try to get someone to adopt him. He's middle-aged, though. It's not easy if they aren't puppies, particularly with this breed. If they can't find someone in a couple of weeks, they'll have to put him down. They just don't have resources to keep many animals there."

"There are places that take them, though. You pay a fee and they feed them and take care of them."

"No-kill shelters. We don't have any on the island." The vet chuckled. "Hell, you could start one. So you want me to make the call?"

Stanton shook his head. "No. He's coming with me."

When Stanton got home, Hanny whined in the crate in the backseat. He parked in the driveway and opened the crate. Hanny needed help to get out of it, and then Stanton carried him inside. Hanny perked up, probably in response to the air conditioning, and Stanton laid him at the foot of the couch and sat down. He had never had a dog. Not growing up, not with his children. A small panic seized him when he realized another living thing was now relying solely on him.

The difference between Hanny in the yard and Hanny now was astronomical. Even his eyes were different, full of some sense of life again, of hope.

Just as Stanton was wondering what exactly a person did with a dog all day, his cell phone rang. He checked the number and didn't recognize it, though it had Seattle's 206 area code.

"This is Jon Stanton."

"Detective Stanton, I'm glad I caught you," a female voice said. "I'm Kristie Wong. I'm a detective with the Seattle Police Department."

Stanton's heart dropped. "Yeah?"

"We, um, we have a situation up here that I thought you might be interested in. A series of bodies was discovered, and we believe one of those bodies might be Elizabeth Stanton."

Stanton sank back into the couch. Hanny, with an effort as though climbing Mt. Everest, rose up onto his legs and crawled onto the couch. Stanton was so surprised he said, "Holy crap."

"Excuse me?" Wong said.

"Not you, sorry. It was a dog."

"Oh. Well, I came across Elizabeth's file in the archives. Looks like she disappeared twenty-seven years ago, is that right?"

"Yes."

"I read some of the reports. They kept mentioning a ten-year-old boy who would come down to the precinct and try to help with the investigation. I assume that was you?"

"It was." Stanton hesitated. "Why do you think… I mean…"

"We found something. A ring. It had the name E. Stanton

engraved on it."

"Where did you find it?" Silence. "Detective, I already know about Reginald Carter. He was Elizabeth's physics teacher."

"Oh, okay. Well, yeah, we found the ring in a little plastic baggie in his basement. In, like, a workbench. We're still identifying the bodies from dental records. So far, we haven't found Elizabeth's but… anyway, I thought you at least deserved the call. If you'd like, I'd be more than happy to have you part of all this. Professional courtesy and all."

"No… I don't know."

She hesitated. "If you have any questions, Detective, please don't hesitate to call me."

"I won't. Thanks."

Stanton hung up and leaned his head back. He let out a large breath, and Hanny did the same.

6

Stanton decided he would take Hanny for a short walk. A quick bout of exercise couldn't hurt, though the vet hadn't specifically told him to walk the dog. Stanton was surprised at how little information the vet had given him when he left. The one thing he'd stressed was that Hanny had been starved of stimulation as well. Stanton needed to spend a lot of time with him and speak in comforting tones but still show the dog that Stanton was the alpha. Stanton, an intellectual nearly his entire life, had never been the alpha of anything, much less a pit bull.

He tied some heavy twine to the dog's collar, reasoning that Hanny didn't have the strength to hurt himself or break away right now, and took the dog out. Hanny stumbled more than he walked, but by the wag of his tail, Stanton guessed he enjoyed himself enormously. They went up the street, said hi to one of his neighbors, and then slowly made their way back home. Hanny collapsed from exhaustion on the patio. After some water and a little more food, he looked about as happy as a dog could look.

Stanton leaned back in his chair, and the two of them watched the waves rolling across the ocean in the moonlight.

In the morning, Stanton realized he hadn't thought through what he would do with the dog while he was at work, so he took Hanny with him. After a quick walk so Hanny could relieve himself, they went to the precinct.

"Oh... my... gosh," Laka said. "That is the cutest dog. Is that the one from yesterday?"

"Yeah."

"I didn't really get to look at him," she said, bending down and offering Hanny her hand. He ran his tongue over the back of her fist as though giving her permission, and she rubbed his head. "What's he doing here?"

"He's mine until I find someone that can take him in."

A tall, lean detective came over and stared at the dog. "Shit, Jon, make sure the locals don't eat him."

"Fuck you, Buster," Laka said.

"Just tell me you guys don't eat dogs and I'll never bring it up again."

Stanton bent down and patted Hanny's head. "Most of the world actually eats dogs. Some cultures think eating pigs is far more disgusting."

Buster grimaced. "Dog's got personality."

Kai poked his head out of his office. "Laka, Jon, caught one over on Benau Street. Drive-by shooting. Suspects in custody."

"Got it," Stanton said. Kai looked down at the dog. "He's just temporary," Stanton added quickly.

Benau Street was an area of the city most locals knew to stay away from. Most of the residents made their money selling drugs. In fact, one of the narc detectives had told Stanton that one out of every four houses on the street was a drug house. But no convictions came from this neighborhood because no one would ever testify against anyone else. Once the convictions dried up, the police stopped making arrests.

The neighborhood seemed incongruous with its surroundings. One of the most beautiful parts of the island circled the neighborhood: a jungle so deeply green that it seemed to glow in the morning sunlight, the trees dappled orange and yellow. The smell of the coffee plantations nearby wafted over, giving the entire neighborhood a semisweet aroma. But the houses themselves were run-down—car parts, mattresses, and other garbage thrown around lawns and driveways.

Stanton stopped in front of a home with two police cruisers and the Special Investigations Section van out front. Laka sat in the passenger seat, and Hanny whined from his crate in the backseat.

"You might as well let him out," Laka said. "I don't think he'd be much safer in that crate if we got into a wreck."

Stanton let him out and tied his new leash to the steering wheel. The dog whined as Stanton walked away toward the home.

"I think you have a new friend," Laka said.

"Great. A friend that can't talk is exactly what I need right now."

Laka took off her long-sleeved shirt, revealing the tribal tattoos that covered most of her body. She wore her T-shirt and a badge dangling from a lanyard around her neck when they ducked under the police tape. "What you need right now is a girlfriend. What happened to that blonde you were dating? The one with the fake tits?"

"She moved faster than I wanted."

"You mean she wanted to have sex?"

Stanton shrugged. "I can't do it."

"I know you're religious and everything, but isn't that a little outdated?"

"I don't think there's any quicker way to ruin your life than being promiscuous." In front of them, on the porch, lay a man with half his head missing.

"Except maybe that," Laka said.

Thick, black blood had pooled around the body like syrup. Brain matter spattered over the wall, and bits of skull dotted the bush next to the porch. Stanton leaned down and looked at the body as a forensic tech snapped photos. He straightened to see the street and saw three young boys, maybe sixteen, leaning against a police car. One of them, an Asian with a black hoodie, looked antsy and kept glancing around. Finally, the officer's attention turned toward one of the other boys, and the Asian kid darted out into the street and away, uncuffed.

Stanton sprinted through the yard and leapt over the neighbor's fence. He dashed across the street as a truck's driver slammed on his brakes and leaned on the horn.

"Where's the cuffs?" Stanton shouted angrily at the dumbstruck officer as he ran past.

Two other uniforms tried to keep up, but they never got near. Stanton was too fast. He dashed in between houses, up onto a back porch, and jumped into the backyard. The boy was fast, too. He leapt over the fence and Stanton followed.

A dog rushed at them from the yard. Both of them ignored it and kept running. The dog nipped at Stanton, who had to pause and make sure the animal wouldn't pounce on him. He backed away, eyes locked on the dog, which growled at him but didn't lunge. Stanton leapt over the fence into the street.

The boy had circled around so they were back on Benau Street, and the kid was at least half a block ahead. Stanton dug in and gave it everything he had. He ran so fast he nearly tripped over the curb, but he didn't stop. His heart pounded in his ears. His lungs burned. But he was gaining.

He saw his Jeep up ahead. The officers were all spread out; no one was positioned to nab the kid, who was clearly headed to the car he'd been pulled over in.

Stanton heard something else, too. Manic barking. Hanny rushed out of the Jeep only to be pulled back by the collar. But the dog didn't give up, either. It rushed forward several times, enough to loosen the leash tied around the steering wheel. The leash came off, and Hanny leapt into the road.

Stanton wasn't far behind the kid now. Instinctively, the dog seemed to know what was happening. Hanny rushed the kid.

The kid pulled out a handgun from the small of his back.

"No!" Stanton shouted.

He closed the distance between them, slamming into him like a linebacker. The gun flew out of his hand and hit the pavement. Stanton lifted his arm and smashed his fist against the kid's face. He did it again and again and again, until the boy's face was covered in blood. He kept punching and stopped only when arms lifted him off the kid and held him back. Two officers and Laka seized him as the kid gurgled and spit.

Stanton breathed heavily, staring down at him, wondering what the hell had just happened.

Stanton sat in his psychiatrist's waiting room, his hand bandaged and swollen to the size of a grapefruit. He had a hairline fracture in his middle knuckle, but that wasn't what bothered him.

After the incident, the Internal Affairs Division had arrived, and he had to give up his badge and gun while they conducted an investigation. Without the gun, something he never used to need, he now felt naked, exposed.

Everyone was interviewed, with Stanton and the initial officer on scene taking the longest. The officer was also the one who had pulled the three suspects over. He knew one of them and his older brother from high school, so he hadn't followed protocol to cuff them and stick them in the backseat or on the curb. He hadn't even searched them for weapons. Stanton was angry with the officer but angrier with himself.

Dr. Vaquer opened her double doors and turned to Stanton. "Come in, Jon."

Stanton sat across from her and stared down at the bandage around his hand. A small drop of blood leaked through the white, like a dab of red dye in a glass of milk.

"I'm not sure you've ever set an emergency session before, Jon."

He swallowed. "I almost beat a kid to death. He was seventeen. I knocked out several of his teeth, broke his nose and his cheek… the only reason I stopped beating him was because people pulled me off."

She was silent a moment. "Did this happen today?"

"Yes."

"Did you dream last night?"

He nodded.

"Please tell me about it."

"I was in some canyon or something. Out in the wilderness. The sky was tinted red. It was just… desolate. But there were remnants of a city, like skeletons of skyscrapers and buildings. I stood in the middle of it."

"What did you feel like? Seeing all this desolation around you?"

"I felt… I don't know if there's a word to describe it. It felt inevitable. That feeling you get when something happens that you knew was coming." He hesitated. "And out of the ground underneath me, something started coming up. A hand. A black hand. It gripped the dirt and the rest of the body crawled out. It was… it was, um…"

"Your sister?"

He nodded.

"Have you ever had this dream before?"

"No. Not like this."

"Did something happen that reminded you of your sister recently? Other than speaking about her here?"

Stanton exhaled and leaned back into the couch. "A detective from Seattle called me. She said they found my sister's ring in that man's house I told you about. Her teacher."

"How did that make you feel?"

"Terrified."

She leaned forward. "I've seen this phenomenon before, in the parents of missing children. Once the child is gone for a long period and the parents have grown accustomed to not having them around, on a very primitive level, unconsciously and completely unaware of it, they often recoil at the thought of finding out what actually happened. It would reopen the wound and start everything over again. The entire healing process would begin anew."

Stanton looked out the window. Across the street, a tree swayed lightly in a breeze, beyond it blue skies with only the faintest hint of clouds. "I don't know if I can do it. My sister raised me. Her death spun my entire existence upside down. The day she disappeared was the day I learned the world wasn't the way my parents described it. To see her remains, to hear the ME talk about how she was likely killed…"

"Jon, I'm not going to lie to you. It will probably be the most painful experience of your life. But the therapeutic value could be astronomical. Think about it: your decision to get a PhD in psychology, to become a police officer rather than an academic, your inability to form long-term relationships with women, that fear you always have that everyone you love will one day just leave… it's all tied together. The lynchpin is your sister."

Stanton suddenly felt heat in his cheeks, and his vision began to blur. "I have to go."

"The session's not over."

"I just need to be alone. Thanks for seeing me, Natalia."

As he reached the door, she said, "Jon?"

"Yeah?"

"If you do decide to go, will you do something for me?"

He turned to her. "What?"

"Will you please remember that sometimes knowing the truth is better, even when it feels like it's not?"

He nodded and left the office.

8

The waves rolled lazily into shore and broke on the soft sand. As the sun set, the ocean turned a dim orange, and most of the surfers called it a day. Some of the locals stayed in the water, splashing around like children in a pool; others sat on the beach and smoked pot out of multicolored pipes, and some just fell asleep on the beach. The tourists went back to their hotels as darkness and the unfamiliar gave them an uneasy feeling.

Most of the islanders were welcoming, but a strong separatist movement led to violence against whites. The derogatory term *Haole,* used for whites, meant something like "invader." Stanton had stopped several beatings on the beaches when white tourists attempted to surf locations the locals felt belonged to them.

Of course, for every movement there was a reaction. A strong white-power movement had built in recent years with a series of successful lawsuits behind it and a growing base of power with whites taking top positions in law enforcement, city government, prosecutor's offices, and county and state administration. The island that had begun as a place of peace and serenity for Stanton was slowly boiling into a cauldron of hate.

But all of that was on his periphery. He'd never experienced violence against himself or his boys when they'd lived there, and he had no desire to join a white power movement. As far as he was concerned, the world had always been and always would be a mess. There was nothing he could do to change much of that mess.

He stared at the water and the harsh reflections of light that broke on its surface. He thought back to the last memory he had of his sister. The night she had gone to the movies with her friends and disappeared, their parents had had a fight. Elizabeth came into Jon's room and sat with him on the bed as their mother and father screamed at each other downstairs.

"Jonny," she'd said, "I don't want you to think this is normal or right. It's not. When people get married, they love each other. Sometimes they just forget that."

Elizabeth gave him a kiss and held him as the screaming continued. When it was over, she headed downstairs, had a few words with their parents that Stanton didn't hear, and left for the movies. That was the last time her family saw her alive.

Stanton rose and got into his Jeep. On the interstate back to his home, he listened to Vivaldi, the wind roaring in his ears. When he finally got home, lights lit up the island like a series of signal fires. He got out and went straight to his patio, where Hanny lay next to a bowl of water. The dog had been sleeping and woke only when Stanton was near. Instantly, he wagged his tail and his tongue darted in and out of his mouth. Stanton sat down in a patio chair and put his foot up on another chair as the dog came over. He rested his chin on Stanton's leg, and Stanton rubbed his head.

"What do you think?" Stanton said, looking down into the dog's soft brown eyes. Stanton held his gaze a moment before the dog looked away. "Yeah, I thought so, too."

Stanton took out his cell phone and searched for the 206 area code in his incoming calls. He hit redial, and it rang four times before it went to voicemail.

"Hi. You've reached Detective Katie Wong. Please leave your name, case number, and the purpose of your message, and I'll get back to you as soon as possible. Thank you."

"Detective Wong," Stanton said, "it's Jon Stanton. I'm going to be booking a flight tomorrow to come up. I would appreciate you keeping me in the loop about anything having to do with my sister... thanks."

He hung up and looked out over the ocean, the dog sloppily lapping at the water in the bowl next to him.

9

In the morning, Stanton sat at his Mac and booked his flight. He didn't want to leave Hanny behind, though ultimately he was unsure whether he was bringing the dog along for the dog's sake or his own.

A pet plane ticket was more expensive than his own, and the dog would have to be kept in the cargo hold. The flight, nonstop, would be just under six hours. Six hours in a dark cargo hold didn't sound like the kind of thing he wanted to put Hanny through. He googled information on pet day cares and found a place not far from downtown that would watch the dog for an extended stay. It even had online access to live feeds, so the owners could check on their pets in real time.

He dropped Hanny off at Good Friends Pet Care. He thought he should rub the dog's head or something, some display of affection, but it felt unnecessary. Instead, he paid with a credit card, told them he'd be back in about a week, and then left. Hanny howled a bit, but it seemed like something any dog would do, and Stanton didn't turn around.

The only other person that had to be notified was Kai. Stanton arrived at the precinct a bit after ten and found Kai already digging into a Spam-and-red-pepper sandwich. Stanton sat across from him and waited a beat before speaking.

"Sorry. I know you don't like people to interrupt you while you're eating."

He shook his massive head. "I've never said that."

"I can tell. Your body posture changes, like you're about to attack."

He shrugged. "I like my food." He put the sandwich down and wiped his fingers with a napkin. "So, what's up?"

"I need to leave for a week."

"Where you goin'?"

"Seattle."

He nodded. "Laka can handle your cases. Let me know when you'll be back."

"Thanks. I appreciate you not asking why."

"I trust you, hoaloha. If you wanted to tell me, you would."

Stanton was about to rise but then felt he owed Kai something. Kai had convinced him to come back to the police force, a lateral hire that let him keep his stripes and stay a detective. He left Stanton alone to work his cases and never bothered him about anything. The least Stanton could do was to be up front with him.

"I never told you this, Kai. I don't want Laka or anyone else to know. You're one of my oldest friends, so I feel I can trust you with it."

Kai's brow furrowed and he leaned forward, understanding that he was about to be told something important. Stanton felt awkward for prefacing his statement now and wished he'd just come out with it.

"When I was ten years old, my older sister disappeared from a movie theater. We knew it was a kidnapping. She wasn't the type to run away or anything like that. After a couple of years, we lost hope we'd ever see her. About a month ago, they discovered several bodies of missing young girls in the former home of one of the teachers from my sister's school. A detective called me and said they'd found something of my sister's there. I just… I think I need to go up there."

Kai nodded, the wrinkles never leaving his brow. "You want me to go too?"

"No. I appreciate it, but no. I think I have to do this alone. I need to know what happened to her. How it all… ended."

Kai nodded again. "You take as long as you need, hoaloha. We'll still be here."

Stanton rose. "I probably won't be longer than a week."

Stanton found Laka at her desk typing up a report. He sat next to her and exhaled. She had a pen in her mouth and occasionally took it out to mark up some notes in a legal pad.

"I'm leaving for a bit," he said, watching her scribble. "Some personal issues. I'll be back as soon as I can."

She returned to typing. "These the type of personal issues you need to talk to someone about?"

He shook his head. "No, I'll be fine. Just something from a long time ago that hasn't closed. Call me if you need anything."

As Stanton got up, she said, "Be careful, Jon. Whatever it is, I'm getting the impression it's not safe."

He grinned. "Nothing is. I'll be back as soon as I can."

10

Returning to the place of his birth filled Stanton's gut with gray dread. Seattle held a lot of memories. His childhood had consisted of few friends and a lot of solitude. Early on, he grew bored in school, and his boredom manifested in cutting school and finding other, more interesting things to spend his time on.

Once when he was nine years old, he sat by the ocean and watched the waves. The beaches in Seattle weren't like the beaches in Oahu. Seattle had a few sand beaches, but the beaches close to him were rock or dirt shores with green-tinted water. Still, the sound of the waves calmed him even back then.

As he'd been sitting there, he noticed something crawling up the beach: a little red crab. Seeing the crab's awkward progress put a smile on his face, until he noticed another crab behind it coming out of the surf, and then another and another. Soon crabs swarmed the beach. Stanton didn't move. He wanted to see what they would do. Would they attack or go around him?

As the crabs neared, his heart pounded and he thought maybe getting mauled by crabs wasn't the best idea. But they were already too near.

Once they reached him, he saw they didn't care one bit that he was there. A few crawled over his legs, but the rest ignored him.

He heard a squeal behind him and saw some other boys with BB guns. Laughing, they lifted the weapons and began firing into the swarms. Green goop spattered as the BBs hit their targets, and the ones that weren't hit were flipped completely over onto their backs. Stanton watched as one baby crab tried to scurry away from the carnage, and one of the boys came over and crushed it with his foot.

"What the fuck you lookin' at, little shit?" the boy said to Stanton.

When the boys had had enough, they left Stanton sitting in a sea of corpses. He stared at the bodies a long time—so long that he missed lunch. When he got home, the only person he told was Elizabeth. She didn't seem to understand, but as he wept in her room, she'd comforted him as she always had.

The plane landed smoothly. The overcast sky gave everything a gray tint. He got his only duffle bag and shuffled off the plane.

He hadn't been at this airport since his family had moved to San Diego. He remembered little about that day but did remember that he'd been hungry and asked his father for a slice of pizza. For some reason that Stanton still couldn't understand, his father had said no and made him wait until they landed to eat—maybe so Stanton had a good association with San Diego from the start.

Stanton rented a Jeep Wrangler and left the airport and then the city. He rolled down the windows and let the cool, wet air wash over him. The farther he got from the city and into the surrounding forests of Chelan County, the more the air carried the scent of pine. The anxiety he felt reentering the county limits nearly overwhelmed him. He had to pull over on the side of the road and take a moment.

Canyons and forest surrounded him, cars zipping past on the road. At the top of one canyon, he saw rock climbers ascending the far side, their colorful ropes standing out like loose strings on a T-shirt. He watched them for a while and then got back on the road.

In the small city of Rosebud, Washington, forty minutes from the airport, a collection of homes sat in a swath of forest exactly as Stanton remembered it from twenty-five years ago. The homes looked like a block of white cake, almost nothing between them. He followed the small road through town until he came to what used to be the local 77 Mart, a gas station that'd had some of the best ice cream in the state. It had been turned into a Starbucks.

Before going to King County and meeting with Detective Wong, he'd had to come here first, to prepare himself for what he was going to see and do. This was where it all started… and ended.

Stanton pulled into the parking lot and went inside. He ordered a milk steamer with chocolate and sat down by the window. The people had changed, and not just their clothing or hairstyles, but their essence. Without cell phones or the internet, Rosebud had been disconnected from everywhere else. Once they had them, though, they saw what fashions were in vogue in Los Angeles and Miami and attempted to copy them. The temperature outside couldn't have been over sixty, yet people wore shorts and sandals with Gucci T-shirts.

But some of the older folks, getting their black coffees to go, still had that rugged essence Stanton remembered. His father had worked in Seattle, and they'd lived out here until Elizabeth's disappearance. A year or so after that, they moved to Seattle, his father telling him he wanted to be closer to his work, though Stanton knew it was because the home held too many memories of Elizabeth.

He drank half the steamer and rose to leave. In the corner, he saw a couple arguing. The woman wept softly as the man spoke, explaining something to her that Stanton couldn't hear. As he left the Starbucks, Stanton wished he could've heard what the man was telling her.

Near the Starbucks was an old warehouse that had been abandoned when Stanton lived here. It was still abandoned, and he wondered if anyone had used it in the twenty-seven years he'd been gone.

Outside it had started to drizzle, and he put on his black leather jacket. The jacket was worn and cracked at the sleeves. His ex-wife, Melissa, had bought it for him almost a decade ago. He got back on the road, rolled the windows up, and drove in the rain to a place that haunted his dreams: his childhood home.

The house at 1276 Parker Lane was white with red trim. When he had stopped at the curb, he stared at it as though he didn't know if it were real. Stanton wasn't sure how long he sat in the Jeep, but when he got out, the drizzle had turned into a downpour. He listened to the drops hit his jacket and bounce away, his hair sliding into his eyes.

A "For Sale" sign hung in the window, and another one stood in the front yard. Stanton stepped up to the front porch hesitantly and peered through the window. The interior was decorated as though the home were still lived in, complete with furniture, photographs on the mantel, and a television. Stanton knocked, but no one answered. He went around the house to the backyard. The gate was open, and he stood on the back porch. Three-foot stone pillars stood on either side of the porch, and Stanton hopped up onto one, grabbed the edge of the roof covering the porch, and pulled himself up to the second-story bedroom window: his old room.

He sat on the porch roof for a moment, impressed that he could still climb up after nearly three decades, and then lifted the window and climbed inside. He had broken the lock on his window so someone couldn't accidently lock it when he had snuck away for his outings or when he wanted to come home early from school. In twenty-seven years, no one had bothered to fix it. That summed up Rosebud in its entirety: no one believing the town would last long enough to warrant fixing anything.

His room was almost exactly the same. Different furniture, of course, and in different locations—he preferred his bed next to the window rather than against the wall as it was now—but the paint, the floors, the scents were all the same. He opened the closet, which was empty, and then moved out into the hall. He leaned on the banister and took in the house.

Photos of a family hung on the walls: a man in glasses with short gray hair and a woman with poufy, dyed-blonde hair. Photos of two children were displayed as well, whose lives Stanton saw in a series of just five photographs: their birth, what he guessed was their first day of school, their wedding, their children, and then their retirement. Each photo was hung neatly over the other in a sequence taking up the wall in the hallway. Stanton examined each before his attention turned to the one room in the home he didn't want to go into: the bedroom next to his—Elizabeth's room.

The hallway seemed to close in on him, and his vision began to darken and fade, closing down to a tunnel. He had had enough panic attacks to know when one was beginning. He sat down on the top step, closed his eyes, and breathed, telling himself to calm down, focusing on the image of the beach on the North Shore as he drifted in with the waves. Early in the mornings, when the sun was just coming up, he liked to pretend he was lost on the ocean and drifting to a beautiful and isolated desert island where he could think without interruption.

His vision returning to normal, his heart rate slowing, Stanton got up and went into Elizabeth's bedroom.

This bedroom was painted a different color than Stanton remembered, and he couldn't recall if his father had repainted it after Elizabeth's disappearance. He sat down on the bed. The carpet hadn't been changed in all that time. For how old and threadbare it was, it had surprisingly few stains. He reached down and touched it with his fingertips—the same carpet his sister had walked on. Then he sat up and quietly stared at the walls.

11

Stanton sat in Elizabeth's room so long the rain had stopped by the time he left. He didn't much care if anyone came home while he sat in her room, but no one did.

He didn't need to see his parents' bedroom, but he did stop in the kitchen and splash some water on his face. He dried himself with a paper towel and glanced at the backyard through the window above the sink.

He wondered if any of his old neighbors were still around. Rosebud didn't have much population mobility. The outside world hardly existed here. When Stanton's family first moved to San Diego, it was as if the entire planet had opened up to him and revealed itself. Before then, the world consisted of a town with a population of less than three thousand.

Stanton left the house through the back door and pushed the button on the doorknob to lock the bottom lock on his way out. The sun shone through the gray clouds, still swollen with rain, as he hiked up the sidewalk. Next door had been an elderly woman named Rosa. She was old even back then and had probably long since died. The next house over was a family whose daughter Stanton had had a crush on. *Monique.* He stopped in front of it for a few seconds, and it brought a grin to his face. All the memories of those awkward moments trying to get Monique's attention, never quite succeeding because he didn't have the courage to just come out and ask her out.

At the end of the block was a house with a nicer lawn—the home of Dale Brown, his wife Jaclyn, and their two boys, Nathan and Niles. Stanton had been Nathan's age but had been close to both of them. The Browns would come over for dinner to his own house frequently, and he remembered that Dale and his own father had been fishing buddies. Nathan had come to Elizabeth's funeral and was the only reason Stanton could be there without having a breakdown. Niles didn't show up to the funeral, which Stanton thought was odd because he and Elizabeth were close.

He went to the front door and knocked. Dale had been a carpenter, and with business doing well, he was sure the Browns didn't live here anymore. It would've been nice to see a familiar face.

A man answered in a plaid flannel shirt tucked into Dockers. The large eyeglasses were new, as were the wrinkles and gray hair, but Stanton recognized Dale Brown. Dale must've recognized him too because his eyes widened, and his jaw nearly fell open.

"Jonny?"

"How are you, Mr. Brown?"

He'd called him Mr. Brown instead of Dale. He thought it odd how people reverted to the rules of authority from childhood. The same reaction had manifested when he was around teachers from his youth.

"I think you can call me Dale now." He opened the screen door and stepped through, setting his hand on Stanton's shoulder. "Boy, you have really taken on your mom's looks, haven't you? A knockout, just like she was."

Stanton, despite himself, blushed. "I'm sorry to bother you. If it's a bad time—"

"What're you, crazy? Come inside. You want some coffee?"

"I'm fine, thanks."

The interior of the home was just as Stanton remembered. Nothing out of place, and there were more photos on the walls. Dale led him into the kitchen and sat him down at the table. He set out two cups of coffee and a plate of pastries before sitting down.

"I'm so sorry about your mama," Dale said. "When I heard about that, it broke my heart. She was such a sweet lady. Always there for everyone that needed it. Cancer sneaks up on you like that, gets the best of us."

Stanton nodded. "Some aboriginal cultures think cancer's a curse on our species for our lack of respect for the earth."

"Shit, you don't need a curse to die, son. Everything in nature's tryin' to kill us." He took a sip of the coffee. "How's your old man?"

"He passed about six years ago."

Though Dale clearly hadn't heard, he didn't seem surprised. His gray eyebrows lowered and he nodded, taking another sip of coffee before staring out the window for a few seconds. "I'm sorry. I hadn't heard. Don't get much news up here, and after you guys moved he didn't really stay in touch."

"My father didn't really understand friendship. He told me friends were just people you could tolerate in short bursts. Everyone else was intolerable."

Dale chuckled. "Yeah, that sounds like him." Dale looked him up and down. "So how you been?"

"I'm good. I've got two kids, Matt and Jon Junior. One's in college and the other's in high school."

"Yeah? Who'd you marry?"

"No one you'd know. I met her in San Diego. We're divorced, though."

Dale took another sip of coffee and then pushed the cup away. "Jaclyn died about ten years ago. I tried to get ahold of your father so you all could come, but he never returned my calls."

"I'm sorry to hear that. She was always kind to me."

"Yeah, well, that's life, ain't it? It gives you somethin' and then takes it away."

Stanton hesitated. "Dale, the reason I'm here is because of Reginald Carter."

Dale's countenance changed. In an instant, anger bubbled up within him somewhere and he grimaced. "Why the hell would you spend even two seconds thinkin' about that no-good son of a bitch?"

"I just—I remembered that you, he, and my father went out fishing a couple of times."

Dale's eyebrows went up. "I see. You think Elizabeth…"

"Yeah."

"I was in such shock when they discovered all them bodies in his house I didn't even connect the dots. It would make sense, I guess. If she was one of them."

Stanton swallowed. "What happened, Dale? How did no one see this?"

"Hell, you knew the guy. Did you think anything was off about him?"

Stanton thought back to his few interactions with Reginald Carter. From what he remembered, his father, Dale, and he had gone fishing twice and out for beers a couple of times. Stanton had met him on the return from one of those trips. He was a tall man, bald, with a wide smile that went from ear to ear. Looking back on it now, he knew he hadn't sensed anything odd about the man. He was active in his church, a high school teacher and coach, and volunteered at the women's shelter—although he had heard his mother comment that it was odd Carter wasn't married by then when he was in his late forties.

"No," Stanton admitted, "I didn't think anything was off about him."

Dale nodded. "That's what I'm talkin' about. He had all of us fooled. I saw this show once about Bind Torture Kill, BTK, that killer in Kansas. They had friends of that bastard on, and they was saying how they didn't see it coming, and he was the last person they would've suspected. I thought it was bullshit at the time. How could you be friends with someone, spend time with them, and not know they was killing people when you weren't around?" He shook his head. "And then all this. Enough to make a man wanna just lock up in his own house and not come out."

Stanton shifted in his seat. "How many were there really? The news said sixteen."

Dale shrugged. "I haven't kept up with the story. The whole thing makes me so sick I just can't stomach it." He ran his finger around the lip of his coffee cup. "But I can see why you'd want to know. Is Elizabeth one of the bodies?"

"They don't know yet. They found her ring in his basement."

He shook his head. "I'm so sorry, Jonny. If I'da known, Lord as my witness, I woulda put a bullet in that son of a bitch's head. I swear it."

"I know." He paused. "I just wanted to see a familiar face, I guess. I'm going to head back up to Seattle. I'll probably be out again soon, though."

"Oh, yeah. I did see the Seattle PD was handling this, not the local sheriffs. Why's that?"

"If a case is too complex, a lot of smaller agencies kick it up to bigger ones. They have more resources and manpower. When you're POST-certified as a police officer, technically you're certified in the entire state, so it doesn't really matter."

"How you know that?"

"I'm a homicide detective."

Dale first looked shocked, and then he chuckled. "You've got to be shittin' me. George Stanton's son is a cop? Your father hated the government in a way no Tea Party flag waver ever could."

"I know. He was less than pleased when I told him." Stanton glanced around the home. "I appreciate your time, Dale. I better get going."

"You haven't touched your coffee."

"I'm Mormon, but I appreciate it."

Dale pushed his glasses back up, eyeing Stanton. "You're just full of surprises, aren't you?"

He grinned. "Sons tend to become the opposite of their fathers or identical to them, I guess. Hey, what's Niles up to nowadays?"

Dale's face sagged and he looked away. "Honestly, I don't really know. We don't talk much. He was a real estate man up in Seattle, but that was 'bout ten years ago. When his mother died, we never talked. Same with Nate."

"I'm sorry."

"Yeah."

Stanton pulled out one of his business cards and wrote his cell phone number on the back. He slid it to Dale and said, "Let me know if you talk to Nate or Niles. Give them my number. I'd love to catch up with them."

He nodded. "Sure thing, Jon. I appreciate you stopping by. Gets lonely sometimes."

"Yeah, me, too."

12

From the interstate, Stanton could see the Space Needle. He remembered it fondly. When his parents had taken Elizabeth there for her fourteenth birthday, some guy climbed out onto the ledge and stole a lightbulb. Nine-year-old Stanton had wondered what it would take for a man to risk his life for a lightbulb. Did he have such joy in life that it made him do things that seemed reckless to everyone else? Or did he hate himself so much that losing his life for something so insignificant didn't really matter?

Within half an hour, Stanton was near the Seattle Police Department. It was one of the most advanced and innovative in the country. Stanton used to teach seminars on forensics and profiling across the country, and the detectives who attended from SPD were always educated and articulate, asking good questions and providing feedback on what they'd like to see in the next seminar.

Some of the most innovative trends in law enforcement had begun there. The broken-window theory that helped clean up New York's streets in the nineties had originated in Seattle. If people thought there was a lot of crime, they would commit more crimes. Researchers had found that the best indicator of the crime rate of a neighborhood had nothing to do with the makeup of the population and everything to do with windows: the more broken windows in a neighborhood, the higher the crime rate. In Seattle, they began fixing broken windows and stationing old police cruisers that were not in use in easy-to-spot locations. Every day, officers would move the cruisers around, giving the appearance that the police were there and watching. Once a week, a crew would go out to the abandoned or run-down buildings and fix the windows. In some neighborhoods, these two tactics lowered crime by almost 40 percent.

Stanton parked in guest parking across the street and crossed the intersection on foot. The sky was still overcast, and it gave him an uncomfortable numbness in his stomach. He always forgot how much he needed sunshine until he visited somewhere that didn't have any.

The interior of the building was clean and modern, with glass used everywhere it could be. Stanton guessed the track lighting was of a luminosity that mimicked sunlight. It made the interior feel airy and elegant.

He waited at the reception desk until the uniformed officer behind it got off the phone and looked up at him.

"What can I do for you?"

"Katie Wong, please."

"She expecting you?"

"Yes, I'm Detective Jon Stanton. Thanks."

Stanton sat down in the waiting area. The magazines, unlike at every police agency he had ever worked for, were all the current issue. He'd begun flipping through a *Scientific American* when he heard the click-clack of high heels on linoleum. He looked up to see a slim woman in a white button-front shirt and a black skirt. She smiled and held out her hand. Stanton shook it.

"Katie Wong."

"Jon Stanton. Nice to meet you."

A small, sympathetic smile moved her lips. "I'm sorry it had to be under these circumstances."

"It's okay. I just want to close this part of my life."

She hesitated. "I'm afraid that might not happen right away, Detective."

"Why's that?"

"Because we've identified all sixteen bodies from Reginald Carter's home. None of them are your sister."

Stanton followed Katie to her office. To his surprise, it actually was an office and not a cubicle like the one he had. She sat down behind a black desk, and he sat across from her. Behind her on a table were a series of photographs of her with a few celebrities, basketball stars and the like. On both ends of the row were photos of her with a young boy, clearly her son.

"How old is he?" Stanton said.

She grimaced and then swallowed. "He would be thirteen this year."

Immediately, Stanton understood he had overstepped his bounds. The boy had died. The look of pain on Katie's face made Stanton nearly wince at his stupidity, though he knew it was an innocent question anyone would've asked. Changing the subject would demean what she had just told him.

"I'm sorry."

She shook her head. "You didn't mean anything by it."

Katie's face had softened, somehow dimmed. The intelligence Stanton had seen when he first met her had waned, and she looked emptier now. She closed her eyes for a moment, feigning a blink. It took just a little too long, but when she opened them again, the hard exterior of her face and the intelligence in her eyes were back.

"I'd like to talk about your sister," she said.

Stanton put his feet squarely on the floor and his hands on the arms of the chair—a posture that had been shown to invoke a sense of trust in those one was speaking with. A posture that exposed one fully to the other person and, on some primal level, the other person responded to. "Dental records?"

Katie nodded. "Yes. We were able to match fifteen of the sixteen through dental records. The last girl, Mindy Deuter, we identified by a spinal deformation she'd had since birth. We ran a search through missing persons for young girls that age with that deformity and got a hit on her. It didn't matter, her mother had died during childbirth, and her father didn't even care. You shoulda heard him. When I called to tell him we'd found his daughter, he had this disdain in his voice, like 'How could you interrupt me just to tell me that?' Really made me sick."

"It matters."

"Excuse me?"

"You said it didn't matter that you identified her. It matters. *She* matters."

Katie hesitated. "I didn't mean it like that. I meant only that we put in a lot of work identifying her and there was no one to tell."

Stanton had seen a shift in many homicide detectives after a few years on the job. The horror of what they had to deal with wasn't a horror people were meant to deal with. Human brains had not evolved to constantly think about death. Many cultures had developed ways to avoid having to think about death. When people were thrust into long-term scenarios where death was all they had to think about, the stress could manifest in many different forms. Alcoholism and sex addiction were two of the most common. Drugs, violent tempers, and suicide were others. To combat this, many homicide detectives simply turned off the empathic part of themselves. They kept the victim at a distance and treated the murder as a puzzle.

Stanton couldn't do that. His mind wouldn't let him. He felt every cut and break the victim felt when he looked at a crime scene and pictured what had happened. His mind had no barriers, and the horror seeped into everything else. Though he knew this made him a better investigator, sometimes there was nothing he wished more than to be able to detach as others could.

"Where did you…" He stopped, the words caught in his throat. He had to swallow and thought about asking for a glass of water but decided it would take too long, allowing him to dwell on the question. "Where exactly did you find the ring?"

"In a locked drawer of a worktable in the basement along with a few other things—gloves and stuff like that. The ring was underneath."

"Were all the girls from the same school? The one Carter taught at?"

"James Moss High School? No. Three were; the rest were from surrounding cities and counties. It would've made more sense for him to choose all the girls from different cities. We don't know why he chose the three he did."

Stanton looked down at the cracked end of a sleeve on his leather jacket. "Because he couldn't stop it. He saw them in class and started fantasizing about them. He became so obsessed with them that that's all he could think about. His mind wouldn't let him do anything else. And then one day he realized he had to take them or go crazy, so he took them. But he felt terrible afterward. I wouldn't be surprised if he tried harder to hide those three. Maybe cut them up or attempt to disintegrate them with lime or acid. Something like that."

Katie was silent a moment. "We found those three bodies buried in the backyard. They were thrust into barrels filled with water and sulfuric acid. He didn't get the mixtures right and the teeth and bones remained intact, so we were able to get IDs."

Stanton exhaled and leaned back in the chair. "I need to see it."

"See what?"

"I need to go to his house."

13

Reginald Carter had lived in Rosebud. Katie offered to drive, so Stanton sat in the passenger seat of her red Prius. He kept his eyes aimed out the window at the raindrops that spattered against the glass and then dribbled down to the door. He watched the neighborhoods as they passed. Buildings and businesses, homes and apartments... all of it built after he'd left. But the vegetation was something else: a luscious green, almost emerald. The farther they got from the city, the greener the leaves and bushes became.

"Did you know Reginald?" Katie asked.

"Yeah, my dad went fishing with him a couple of times. There aren't a lot of people in Rosebud. Everyone knew everyone else."

"Is your dad still around? I'd like to talk to him."

"No, he passed away from a coronary. My mother died a couple of years before that."

"Sorry."

Stanton looked at her. She drove with her hands in perfect formation on the wheel: two o'clock and ten o'clock. She seemed rigid while she drove, nervous. "Have you notified all the families?"

"Yeah. Me and my partner, Thomas. We split the sixteen down the middle and did it in one afternoon. It's the part of this job I like the least." She glanced at him. "I read that you're Homicide, too. That true?"

"It is."

"Must be pretty laid back in Hawaii."

"There's actually quite a bit of murder, considering how small the islands are. Most are domestic violence related or drug deals gone bad, things like that. But California, for some reason, is a magnet for serial murderers. They usually stop going west once they hit there."

When the car entered Rosebud, that familiar numbness in his stomach was back. Though the rain had stopped, the sky sucked light into its deep gray, giving the appearance of night falling though it was the middle of the day.

Katie remembered where Reginald Carter's house was without having to look it up. It was a big place, at least for Rosebud—one Stanton had seen dozens of times in his childhood and never considered for a moment. Now he knew that Reginald had bought the larger home for the privacy a large basement would provide.

Katie opened her door. "You ready?"

Stanton inhaled deeply and let it out through his nose. He opened the door and stepped outside with his eyes never leaving the house.

A uniformed officer stood guard. Stanton glanced at Katie. "We've been getting people trying to steal things. Serial-killer groupies. They'll take stuff and sell it on eBay. Some keep it themselves. The kind of people who marry serial killers in prison, I guess."

Stanton stood in the small vestibule leading into the home. Plastic now covered some of the furniture, but he could still see a fireplace, a dining table with six chairs, a plant... everything in its place. Normal, except for the living room.

Most of the walls there had been torn open. Stanton guessed the police hadn't found anything. The upstairs was the portion of the house Carter wanted presentable: his face to the world. The basement would be where he really lived.

Stanton passed through the living room and stopped in the kitchen. He wondered if Elizabeth had been dragged through this place and to the stairs leading down. If she had screamed and fought... Or had she been unconscious and carefully brought in late at night when none of the neighbors were awake?

The thoughts, for a moment, were detached curiosities. And then the pain of the images flooding his mind pierced him, and he had to stop, to turn it off for a moment. He closed his eyes and thought of the beach, of the surf breaking along the shore on a clear morning. Then he opened his eyes and continued through the house.

The stairs leading down to the basement seemed freshly carpeted. Stanton reached down and touched the carpet. It felt rigid, as if it hadn't been used much, with no visible stains. The police hadn't torn up the stairs yet. He would have to make sure they did that.

After a few steps down, he paused and looked up at Katie. "Did they find photographs or videos?"

"Of the girls? No. Why?"

"Those three you found in the barrels. I think he would've kept something more than jewelry or their school IDs. He would've wanted something that he could look back on and masturbate to."

She was silent a second and then said, "No, nothing that we saw."

"Huh," Stanton said, turning back toward the stairs. He kept his eyes on the stairs until he was on the bottom step and then looked up. The pain of it stung him like a needle in the chest. Was this really the last place Elizabeth saw alive? It was so… depressing. Hanging lightbulbs that moved slightly with a breeze from an open window that had been painted black, worktables and benches, tools hanging on the walls, metal cupboards, a few hunting trophies—the heads of bucks— mounted and stacked against the wall. A place as dark and dreary as Stanton had ever seen. If this was the last place Elizabeth ever saw, she must've been absolutely terrified.

Stanton's heart sank, and he felt the familiar dizzy sensation that preceded the tunnel vision and, occasionally, the passing out. He sat down on the bottom step, his chin in his hands as he took in every inch of the basement. Every corner, every crack in the cement floor, every nail in the wooden beams.

"Do you wanna see where we found the ring?" Katie asked from behind him.

"No," he said.

This is my refuge, Stanton thought. *This is my refuge and place of wonder. The one place in the world where I'm king. These girls wouldn't give me a second glance during the day, but here, I am a god to them. They worship me… and I allow them to worship me. I keep them alive as long as I can, as long as they're able, but I have to see it… I have to see the look in their eyes when they know they're going to die. That look is what I live for. It's what this is about.*

Stanton rose. "I think he has photos or video of the moment they die. It's gotta be somewhere here."

Katie leaned against the wall. "I told you, we've torn the basement apart. Didn't find anything like that."

"What's in that room off to the side?"

"Stacks of garbage. We're still making our way through it all."

"Some people keep a mess room where they dump everything that doesn't seem to fit somewhere else. You see it a lot in the homes of drug addicts. Do you have a pair of latex gloves?"

She took a step down. "Jon, I appreciate that you're a detective, and I'll help you as much as I can, but I can't let you go rifling through evidence. Even bringing you, the family member of one of the victims, down to the crime scene could get me in trouble if this ever went to court. Could you imagine what a good defense attorney would do with that?"

Stanton watched her as though she were a curiosity. How could she be so passive about this? This place had been hell to more than a dozen young girls. How could she not want to do everything in her power to figure out why this happened? It was something he never could understand in others. His wife used to beg him to quit police work because of the psychological toll it took on the family, and he couldn't understand why she was willing to make that sacrifice. Maybe it was better not knowing what was out there, and they didn't want that ignorance taken from them.

"Defense attorney for who?" Stanton said. "He's dead, Katie. It doesn't matter what happens now."

She hesitated. "Just lemme make sure everything in there's been photographed before you start going through it."

14

The CSI unit had finished photographing everything in the house days ago, but just to be sure, Katie had a couple of forensic techs go through the mess room and take video and a handful of photos. When they were done, she got some latex gloves from them and handed them to Stanton, who snapped them on and stood over the pile of junk.

Stacks of envelopes, letters, discarded food containers, and empty cans and bottles took up the entire room. In the center of the room, the largest pile sat like some volcano ready to explode. Stanton got onto his hands and knees and began going through it. Something in this house would lead him to the photos or video he was looking for. He was certain of it. He'd bet anything on it. If he'd learned anything about men like Reginald Carter, it was that a little of something pleasurable wasn't enough. They had to drag the momentary pleasure out as long as they possibly could. He wouldn't have been surprised if the girls had been kept alive for weeks down here instead of days, and even then, Carter might've kept the corpses a bit longer.

Most of the envelopes were bills and advertisements. A few letters from old friends and family, people from another generation where writing a letter seemed like a practical way to give someone a message. Stanton read them all. One from Carter's mother described her disappointment in him because he wasn't married. She had a nice girl in her church congregation who'd be perfect for him. Another, also from his mother, asked why he hadn't come to his father's funeral.

"We haven't catalogued it all," Katie said, folding her arms, "but we've sifted through it. There's no photos in there."

"If you've searched the house and they weren't here, they've got to be somewhere else."

"Like a storage unit? We thought of that. Ran his name and didn't find one."

Stanton shook his head, though he wasn't looking at her. "He wouldn't use his own name."

The pile seemed to widen as Stanton sorted through it. Beads of sweat formed on his forehead and trickled down, and he wiped them on the back of his arm.

Katie had left for a long time, and when she returned she said, "We should probably go soon."

Stanton turned to her. "I'd like to stay if that's possible."

"No way. I can't leave you here, and I've got to get back. I've got other cases…" She paused, probably remembering that she wasn't just talking to a cop but to someone who had lost a loved one in this house. "I'm sorry. I didn't mean it to come off like that."

"No, I understand. Can I just have five more minutes?"

She smiled sadly, as though catering to a child who didn't understand how the world worked. "Sure."

Stanton quickened his pace, going through every letter, every scrap of paper. Something was here. Something he needed. He developed a rhythm as he pushed envelopes around and threw advertisements on the other side of the pile away from him.

Nearly at the bottom of the stack, he saw an unopened envelope from a bank. He took it out and held it in his hand for a moment before carefully tearing the top and slipping the letter out. It was a statement for Reginald Carter's credit card, from almost five years ago. Near the middle of the description of charges was one for four dollars to Alcatraz Storage. Stanton rose. He glanced back at Katie, who was speaking to one of the forensic techs about some training they had attended together.

Stanton folded the slip of paper and placed it in his jacket pocket. He turned around and said, "I'm ready to go."

The forensic tech, a man with shaggy brown hair, said, "Nothin', huh? I'm not surprised. The ME said one of the bodies was at least twenty years old. This dude got away with killing people for two decades. He had to know what he was doing."

Stanton brushed past him wordlessly, and Katie said good-bye and followed him. When they were back outside and walking to the car, Stanton said, "You think there's any way I could see the autopsy reports?"

"You know I can't release that. The victims' families could sue."

"The families want this done with as soon as possible. If you want, I could call them and explain it. Have them sign a waiver."

She got into the driver's seat of the car and unlocked the passenger door for him. "I think it has to end here. I'm sorry. But I know what I'm doing, too. I'll do everything I can to find out why your sister's ring was in that house."

Stanton turned his eyes toward the road. "Thanks."

15

Katie gave Stanton her card with her number written on the back before dropping him off at the precinct. She waited until he got into his Jeep and drove away then stepped out of her car and headed inside. She felt bad that this was how he had to find out about his sister's final moments in some dark, wet basement. And on top of feeling bad for him, she could also sympathize with him. Part of the reason she wanted him gone was that seeing that pain in his eyes, that willingness to do anything and everything to get an explanation about his sister, brought up painful memories of her son.

Her partner, Thomas Garcia, sat in the bull pen, talking with other detectives. The laughter died down when she neared, and she knew they'd been talking about women.

"Where were you?" Thomas asked.

"Reginald Carter's house. Just tying up some loose ends."

"Why would you go back there?" he said, taking a sip of coffee out of a Styrofoam cup.

She shrugged. "It's done now. I don't need to go back again."

Katie turned and headed to her office. Before she could even shut the door, Thomas was there. He stepped in and shut the door behind him.

"What's up?" he said.

"Nothing. Why?"

"Don't bullshit me," he said, flopping onto the small leather couch against the wall. "I know when something's going on."

She sighed and sat down at her desk, putting her feet up on the footstool she'd received as a Christmas present from her mother. "I took one of the victims' family members there."

"Seriously? What for?"

"The ring we found. Elizabeth Stanton. I took her brother there. He's Homicide, too, out in Hawaii. He wanted to look around."

"At what? She wasn't one of the bodies."

"Thomas, don't be a dick."

He stood up and stretched his back. "What're you doin' tonight? We're goin' out for drinks."

"I'm good," she said, opening up a file on her desk. She waited until he left before closing the file and leaning back in her chair. Why had she taken Jon to Carter's house? She'd never done that for anyone before. And now, somehow, she felt guilty for not giving him the medical examiner's reports when he'd asked. Why would she care about that at all?

She rose from her desk and paced the room a few times before deciding she needed to head home for a quick late dinner.

Occasionally she would eat out for lunch and dinner, but nowhere near as much as the other detectives in her squad. For them, it was some ritual they needed to de-stress. For her, it was the opposite: social situations and a lot of people in a room always gave her anxiety.

She drove slowly with the windows down. The temperature had increased to lukewarm, but the rain had stopped and at least some of the clouds had dispersed. Originally from Michigan, she had no problem with Seattle's weather and had never really had her moods linked to the sunshine as she'd seen in some other people.

Her apartment building was brown and only three stories. She lived on the basement floor and when she walked in, her cat, Patty, lay on the kitchen counter. Katie crossed the living room and kitchen and rubbed the animal's belly, releasing a series of purrs. She opened her fridge and made a salad of couscous, onions, and tomatoes with spinach.

When the salad was done, she set it on the table and stared at it. Eating was the last thing she felt like doing right now. A heavy, tight feeling sat in her gut and wouldn't leave. It was guilt. She knew the feeling and knew what was causing it.

Not that long ago, she had been Jon Stanton—scrambling from government agency to government agency, hoping the next one had the information she was looking for, praying someone friendly would pick up the phone when she asked about her son's death. Katie looked over at the photograph of Brian on the counter next to the microwave. Every room had a photo, as did her office and her car. It'd been six years now, and she knew what people thought: that the grieving had gone on too long. Her own aunt had said as much. *What the hell did she know?* She hadn't lost someone she loved. She couldn't possibly relate to what that did to a person, to how it made her feel when she got up in the morning and, for a fraction of a second, forgot what had happened and still expected Brian to be in his room, and the crushing weight when she remembered she'd never see him again. No one knew what that was like unless they'd gone through it. As she had. As Jon Stanton had.

She pulled out her phone and dialed the ME's office.

16

As Stanton drove away from the police precinct, he realized he didn't have a place to sleep. He hadn't booked a hotel or even thought about where he should stay. He googled the nearest hotels, and the Marriott was closest, on a steep hill near downtown Seattle. A valet took his Jeep, and he checked in and went up to his room.

One of his windows looked out on the ocean. But the ocean here was not the ocean in Oahu. Here it was gray and foreboding, churning violently. In Oahu, the ocean welcomed him like an old friend.

He kicked off his shoes and lay back on the bed before pulling out the credit card statement from Carter's house. On his phone, he found Alcatraz Storage was about twenty-five miles away from Rosebud. He slipped the statement back into his pocket, rose and checked the mini-fridge, decided against the twelve-dollar bottle of water, and put his shoes back on before leaving the room.

The sky had cleared somewhat, but a dull grayness still enveloped the city. While the valet retrieved his Jeep, he stood in front of the hotel and stared at his reflection in a small stream of water flowing down the pavement.

Once in the Jeep, he rolled the windows down again and checked his GPS before getting onto the interstate.

Washington had some of the most beautiful scenery he'd ever come across. Lush, green trees and grass dotted with white-capped mountains and clear rivers and streams. But Seattle itself was like any other city: crowded, polluted, and with the distinct smell that could only be found where great masses of humanity congregated: smog and exhaust, with notes of mildew.

The interstate was relatively clear, and it was a straight shot to the storage unit in Buxton. Once Stanton pulled into the town and found Alcatraz Storage, he was convinced Buxton was even more backwoods than Rosebud. The only place of any note in the town appeared to be a gas station with a Burger King attached. Just out of curiosity, he found the city on Wikipedia and saw that it had fewer than four hundred residents. The contrast amazed him: it was less than two hours from Seattle and yet felt like a different country.

The storage units were gray brick with orange metal doors. Surrounded by a metal gate, video cameras, a security guard, and an alarm system, the storage units were as protected as most banks. Stanton parked and walked to the front office. Soft country music played, and an older woman in a flower-print shirt sat behind the desk. She glanced up at him but didn't say anything. To be polite, Stanton quietly waited until she was ready.

"Yes?" she finally said, not looking up from whatever form she was filling out.

Stanton took out his badge and held it out, waiting. She looked at the badge, then at him. The Seattle PD badge was silver as opposed to the gold and blue Honolulu PD badge Stanton had shown her, but she didn't seem to notice and didn't ask to look any closer.

"What can I do for you, Officer?" she said.

"I have a man who has a storage unit here. I wouldn't expect that he used his own name, but he did use his own credit card. The card on file would be for Reginald Carter with an address in Rosebud. You mind looking that up for me?"

"You have a warrant? Cause I can't let you search without a warrant."

Stanton leaned forward on the counter. "See, the thing is, I could go get a warrant right now, but that's going to take me at least three hours. And I've got better things to do than search some storage unit. I'd rather just get this outta the way, file my report, and we can both go back to our lives. If I get the warrant, I gotta bring other officers down here and we might have to search more than just his unit. I just want in and out."

She stared at him a moment. "In and out, huh?"

"That's right."

She exhaled. "Fine. In and out." She turned to her computer and said, "You got the card number?"

Stanton handed her the credit card statement. She typed it into the company's software and a page of information came up.

"That card's linked to a unit leased by Reagan Cliff... oh, the R and the C, huh?"

"That's right. I'll just bet that's him," he said with a smile.

She smiled back, impressed with her own cleverness. "All right, well, lemme go open her up. In and out, right?"

"That's right."

Stanton followed the woman through the offices to a back door leading to the storage units. She grabbed some keys out of a locked drawer and led him up one of the rows before turning left down another long series of storage units.

"My brother wanted to be a cop," she said.

"That so? Why didn't he?"

"Had some pot convictions back in the seventies. Ain't that the stupidest thing you ever heard? Man can't serve his community 'cause he smoked some dope when he was nineteen?"

"It certainly is."

She shook her head. "This country's goin' to hell." She stopped, looked around, then walked up to a unit and unlocked it. She reached down and lifted the door with a grunt of effort, rolling it to the top.

"This is it," she said.

"Thank you. I'll be out of here as quickly as I can."

"Uh huh," she said, returning to the office. "Just pull down the door when you're done and I'll come out and lock it."

When she'd left, Stanton turned on the single lightbulb in the space. Piles of junk sat a couple of feet deep: another mess room. He wished he'd brought latex gloves with him, but he hadn't even been sure he'd be let in, much less that he'd find anything. So, without the gloves, he began kicking aside the piles of trash with his foot. Within a few minutes, he was down on his hands and knees sifting through the old trash.

Very quickly he saw that it was nothing but refuse—discarded items like fast-food bags that Carter brought with him and didn't bother taking out to a trash bin. Stanton rose and looked over the space. Against the walls were some filing cabinets and several school desks for junior high or high school kids. He walked over to the first filing cabinet; it was locked. He set his shoulder against the edge, gripped the handle on the first drawer, and pulled and pushed at the same time. The force tore out the rickety drawer, revealing papers and file folders. Stanton flipped through them. The papers consisted of descriptions:

Five four, a hundred and five pounds, blonde hair with purple highlights. Has softball practice Tuesdays and Thursdays and Cheer Monday, Wednesday, Friday. Parents divorced, lives with mother who works 11a.m. to 11p.m. Monday thru Thursday. A boyfriend. Boyfriend has swim practice…

The entries went on and on, even going into what they liked to eat and drink. No names, birthdays, or any information that could identify who he was referring to were written anywhere. They had to have been memorized. Stanton counted two hundred and eighty-seven files. He'd memorized the lives of two hundred and eighty-seven young girls over the course of two decades so that he could better pick the right ones. Just off this information, Stanton didn't see a pattern. He couldn't tell why one girl was chosen and another not—not yet, anyway. But the pattern was there. And when he found it, he would understand Carter's obsession, and why Elizabeth was chosen.

He pulled the drawer out completely and reached down into the next one, unlocking it from the inside. When he opened this one, his heart beat faster and he lost his breath.

Stacked in neat little piles were Polaroid photos. No drives to save the photos, just the Polaroids—something Stanton hadn't seen since he was a kid. The top photo was of a young girl, maybe fifteen, screaming, nude, and tied down to the metal table Stanton had seen in Carter's basement.

The photos were caked with dust, and Stanton decided he couldn't handle them without latex gloves. Also, if he happened across a photo of Elizabeth like that… it would be too much. He needed time to prepare himself.

He stepped outside and looked around before rolling the door down. Back at the office, the woman was working on the form again and looked up without saying anything.

"I'm going to need some supplies. I'll be right back," he said.

"Supplies for what?"

He stepped close to the woman. "I'm going to go ahead and assume you didn't know there were photographs of dead children in that storage unit, and you're going to go ahead and not ask me any questions. Because if I thought for a second that you knew what was in there and didn't call the police, that would be felony obstruction of justice, maybe even accomplice to murder. Understood?"

The woman swallowed. She looked as though she wanted to say something but didn't have the courage. Instead, she just went back to her form and said, "Do whatever you want. I don't give a shit."

The closest store was a twenty-four-hour pharmacy. The lighting in those places always gave Stanton headaches, and he moved quickly to avoid staying in there for any length of time. He bought a box of latex gloves and some ibuprofen and left.

He got back to the storage unit and walked past the woman without a word. Other than a quick glance in his direction, she didn't say anything, either. He stood outside the storage unit, held his breath as long as he could, then slowly released it before rolling up the door and stepping inside. He carefully made his way over to the filing cabinet, snapped on some gloves, and then began thumbing through the photos.

They were about as horrible as he'd imagined on the drive over. Moments of agony caught on film for Carter to revel in later. Stanton counted twenty-one girls, which meant Carter hadn't buried them all at his house, or the police hadn't searched thoroughly enough. He got to the bottom of the stack. No photos of Elizabeth.

As he went to put the photos back down, something caught his eye. It was in the middle of the stack. He stared at the photo. A blonde girl with wavy hair was on the metal table, her face contorted in pain. Her arms were tied over her head, but what drew Stanton's attention were her feet. The photo was a body shot, taken from above her, either on a chair or a ladder. Her feet were included. And over the ankles, something covered them. Stanton squinted and stepped closer to the lightbulb to make out what it was.

Hands.

Someone was taking the photo, and someone was holding her down. There were two of them.

17

Painstakingly, Stanton went through every photo several times under the light. Only one other photo had a body shot taken from above. It wasn't as clear in this photo, but he could see the tips of fingers on her ankles. He placed the photos back in the drawer.

He knew he couldn't leave them here. Not while the police thought there were only sixteen victims. The parents of those other five girls deserved to know what happened. Or did they? Maybe their lives were better not knowing. Better having a sliver of hope that somewhere, their little girls were still alive. Stanton didn't know if that was true. All he knew was that he would want to know.

Rolling down the door, he turned to see the woman hurrying toward him, shaken, wringing her hands. "I didn't know anything that was in there. I don't know what's in any of these."

"The police will be here soon. Let them see what's in the storage unit." Her eyes widened. "You won't get in any trouble," Stanton quickly added.

He turned away from her and dialed Katie's cell phone number from the back of her card.

Stanton sat across from the storage unit and leaned his head back against another, his eyes glued on the sky, waiting. He had forgotten how deeply gray the clouds would get here, a gray unlike any he had ever seen before. Staring at it, he felt as if it could suck him up into the sky. As much as he liked Seattle, he knew he couldn't spend too much time there. His mood had always been affected by how much sunshine he got. Whether it was seasonal affective disorder or something else, he couldn't go without the sun for very long.

Katie was the first to arrive, two police cruisers not far behind her. Stanton didn't rise as Katie and a Hispanic man in an expensive suit hurried up to him. Her partner barked, "What the hell? You go rifling through our evidence like some fucking rookie? What if I came down to Hawaii and did that shit to you?"

"Thomas," Katie said, "it's all right. Jon told me he didn't touch anything important without gloves."

"How do we know? What if CSI finds his prints in there? How we supposed to explain that in the news?"

"They'll find my prints on some of the trash, nothing else," Stanton said. He rose, facing the man squarely. "I didn't know if I had anything until I looked. I didn't want to call you out and waste your time if there was nothing in there."

Thomas swallowed, his face turning red from either embarrassment or anger he was holding back. He turned away and stormed over to the storage unit, barking orders at the uniforms coming out of the police cruisers.

Katie took a step forward, lowering her voice. "Why didn't you call me?"

"I did."

"You know what I mean."

Stanton looked over at the storage unit as the uniforms fumbled with the light. "I had to look for myself first," he said. "I needed to be alone in there for a minute."

"Jon, this isn't your investigation. I told you that."

"Is there anyone that has more invested in this than I do? If there is, I'll step aside."

She sighed and glanced over her shoulder. "It doesn't look good for us. What would your boss think if a vic's family member kept showing up at crime scenes?"

"I'm not looking to get in your way, I'm really not. But I know how these are worked. This is a high-profile case. The administration is going to want it cleared and closed as fast as possible. They don't want any messes when the news crews have their eyes on them. They're not looking for additional evidence, and anything you present to them is going to be mocked and set aside."

"What're you talking about? I don't know how it works in Hawaii, but no one puts pressure on us. We work the cases how we see them."

He shook his head, his eyes never leaving one of the uniforms as he joked with another officer about something. "That's not how any government agency works. The top runs the show and only lets you think you're independent. When you tell them anything not in line with their plan, they'll turn on you."

"What would I tell them that's not in line with their plan? Carter's dead. The cases will be closed as soon as CSI's done at the house."

Stanton hesitated. "The case isn't done. Inside one of those filing cabinets is a stack of photos. Old Polaroids. Twenty-one girls, all taken at Carter's house. Two of the girls have something you need to see in the photos."

"What?"

"I don't want to bias you. I want to know that you see what I see. Just look through the photos. I'll be at the hotel."

As Stanton strode to his Jeep, her partner hurried up to him and walked beside him. "Katie's got a soft spot. That's about what I'd always expect from a woman, but don't expect that from me. Vic's family or not, I see you at another one of my crime scenes, you're leaving in cuffs."

Stanton climbed into the driver's side of his Jeep and slipped on his sunglasses. "This wouldn't have been your crime scene if I hadn't found it. You're welcome."

He started the Jeep and pulled away, watching the man stare at him in the rearview.

18

The hotel room seemed smaller as Stanton lay on the bed. He slept at least a few hours, though he couldn't be sure how long since he hadn't looked at the clock when he first lay down.

Glancing out the window, he saw the abysmal grayness of the weather had turned to a deep night, and he turned away from it, onto his side. He closed his eyes and hoped he could sleep a little longer but knew it wouldn't come. So instead he rose, dressed, and headed out to find something to eat.

The hotel had a small grill, and he scanned the menu. A few items looked good, but he wanted to be somewhere less conspicuous. He found the nearest diner on his phone and drove there, in what looked like a residential neighborhood.

Stanton parked on the street and went inside. A booth by the window was open, and he sat down. He hadn't even ordered yet when his cell rang. It was Katie.

"This is Jon."

"Holy shit."

Stanton breathed out. "I'm glad you saw the same thing."

"It could just be him and he set up an automatic photo."

"Maybe. You willing to take that risk and leave it alone?"

A pause. "No."

"Me neither. Katie, I'm not trying to step on any toes, but I can help with this. Carter's the type of perp I specialize in—the ones who have no discernable motive. And it doesn't mean I don't trust you or you're not good at your job. It just means I have something to offer."

"I know. I googled you." She exhaled loudly. "I may catch shit for this, but okay. You can help. Any ideas on where to start?"

"The basement couldn't have been the only place Carter's real personality came out. He had to have been living another life. Maybe involved in the child porn communities. That's probably where I'd start."

"Well, where are you? I'll come pick you up."

Stanton climbed into the passenger seat and buckled himself in.

Katie set several files on his lap. "The autopsy reports—the four we have done, anyway."

"Thanks," he said, putting them on the floor by his feet.

"So where to?"

"Most child porn communities have a hub. We need to find one here."

"What's a hub?"

"You never worked Special Victims?"

"No, I came up from property crimes."

Stanton glanced out the window at a homeless man standing on the corner. "A hub is someone who amasses child porn, or maybe even makes it himself, and then distributes it in email lists to other pedophiles who requested it. You can only get on the list by word of mouth, so it's harder for law enforcement to break in. But it's not done anonymously. A good hub knows who they're dealing with to make sure it's not cops. Find the hub, and we can find everyone on his list."

"But they can email anywhere, right?"

"They can. Child pornographers are much more sophisticated than when the internet first came out. They tend to keep it within state lines now to avoid federal intervention. The FBI's a lot more organized and efficient than most local law enforcement agencies, so by keeping them out, the pedophiles have a much better chance of staying out of law enforcement's crosshairs."

She headed for the interstate. "I didn't know these guys were so elaborate in spreading child porn around."

"A lot of hubs adopt children, rape them for a number of years, and film it. When they're too old, they get rid of them and adopt more children. They study how to get away with it, how to avoid detection and prosecution. They're one of the most dangerous types of predators because they know how atrocious what they do is. A pot dealer thinks what he's doing isn't a big deal. But a hub knows he's a monster, and he doesn't care."

The interstate grew busier and came to a standstill several times due to an accident up ahead. Stanton grew impatient and wanted to read through the autopsy reports but decided to hold off. He wanted to be alone when he read them. Somewhere quiet. The autopsy reports told a story, and to hear the story, he would need to concentrate.

They pulled up to the precinct and went inside. Katie led him through the corridors to a unit marked "Special Victims." Several detectives sat around typing or speaking on the phone, chewing pens and erasers. Many police agencies kept Special Victims detectives, who dealt with sex crimes, on a two-year rotation. The stresses were so great that anything more than two years had been found to cause issues like chronic depression, alcoholism, and paranoia.

A man in a blue button-front shirt sat at his computer. He smiled as Katie stood in front of him.

"I heard about Jacobs," he said. "Nice work."

"Thanks." She waited a second before speaking again. "Greg, we need a favor. This is Jon Stanton. He's with Homicide in Honolulu, and he's helping on the Reginald Carter cases."

Greg looked at him now. "Helping?"

"Just watching," Stanton said.

Katie added, "We were looking for someone known as a hub. You know what that is?"

Greg leaned back in his seat and studied them. "What do you need a hub for?"

"I can't talk about that right now," Katie said, "not until I know for sure."

Greg's brow furrowed. "Okay. Well, *that's* not weird or anything."

She grinned. "Sorry, but I promise as soon as I know for sure, you'll know."

Greg inhaled deeply and let it out through his nose. "Who you lookin' for?"

Stanton said, "It's going to be someone within the state who's been working a long time. Decades. And he was probably busted at some point for massive distribution, like hundreds of thousands of images and videos, or he was found to be raping his adopted daughter or son."

"We got a lotta guys like that."

"I'd appreciate if we could get a list."

He nodded. "I'll email it to Katie."

"Thanks."

Stanton waited until Katie left first. He followed her through the corridors and back outside. Katie waited until they were in the car before speaking. "Sorry," she said. "He was a little standoffish."

"No, he was fine. They have the most stress of any detectives in there. They have the right to be cranky sometimes." He paused. "I didn't actually get to eat. You hungry?"

The restaurant was a local place serving, according to the sign, the best cheesesteaks in the state. Stanton ordered a meatball sub and Katie got a cheesesteak. They sat down at a table with a red-and-white checkered tablecloth. A photo of a famous chef with his own reality show was up on the wall, hugging the chef in the kitchen.

Stanton bit into the sandwich, the marinara sauce dripping down onto the paper plate. "This is awesome," he said.

"Chef Joseph knows what he's doing. He actually learned to make these in prison. He was there for a drug charge, and when he got out, he scraped together some money and started this place."

"Cops always know the best places to eat," he said. "When I was on a beat, it seemed like that's what we did most to fill the time."

"Now they got iPads to watch movies while they wait for calls. Different world." Katie took another bite and put the sandwich down.

"I don't know how you found that storage unit, but I'm guessing it involved obstructing an investigation, so I'm not going to ask."

"I appreciate it."

"But I want everything up front. No more hiding things."

Stanton took another bite. "I promise, no more."

"I do wanna know what you thought you were looking for. You couldn't have guessed there was someone else involved."

"No, I didn't. I was looking for anything that told me what happened to my sister. I suspected he might've buried other bodies in the woods before he started taking them to his house. Maybe put them in Puget Sound or something."

"Twenty-one girls," she said, shaking her head. "Gone just like that. And for what? So he could get off for a few hours?"

"What he did is tied to sex, but it's not about sex. Not really."

"What then? Some deep, subconscious desire that comes from his childhood? That always sounds like a load of bull to me."

"That's not what I believe it is."

"Then what?"

"The devil."

She chuckled, nearly spitting out her food. When she saw he was serious she stopped and took a sip of her drink. "You can't mean that."

"I don't joke about that."

"I've never believed in superstition. If you can't see it, it ain't there."

"Have you ever loved anyone?" Stanton asked.

She hesitated. "Of course."

"Can you see love? Can you hold it or touch it? You can't, but I bet you knew it was real. You knew it was there." He wiped his lips with a napkin. "There's a lot of things in this universe we don't understand yet. The devil is one."

She leaned back in her seat. "So like, a pitchfork and brimstone?"

"No. Just… darkness. Pure black. Nothingness. A feeling that the universe is empty and cold, meaningless. That's all it takes to make a good man bad—a slight shift in perspective, with a nudge from the darkness."

She folded her arms, her eyes glued to her plate for a long time before she said, "When I lost Brian… when I lost my son, I looked for some meaning behind it. Something that could explain to me why it had to happen. He was hit by a drunk driver while playing in front of our house. You know what I found after searching for six years? I found randomness. It's all just random. There's no more design to it than a storm."

Stanton chose his next words carefully. "I'm not saying I understand what God wants of us or why he makes innocent people suffer, but there is something else. You've felt love, then you have to have felt the opposite, that cold darkness just on the periphery. The man who killed your son—"

"It was a woman."

"The woman who killed your son had demons haunting her. I bet if you asked her why she would risk driving after knowing she was drunk, she wouldn't have an answer. People destroy themselves and everyone around them and they don't even know why."

Katie shook her head. "She was evil, that person. But she was just a biological entity, not some force of nature. It doesn't work like that. I wish it did. I wish I had one place to put my anger, but I don't. I blame that woman's parents for letting her drink when she was a teenager, I blame the alcohol companies that advertise on TV and make drinking look glamorous, I blame the bar that served her the drinks, the friends who let her drive home… and most of all I blame her. That she didn't think for a second how many people would be hurt because she didn't want the hassle of calling a cab."

Stanton sat quietly, watching her. Katie's face had flushed red and her breathing had increased. Stanton saw pain emanate from her face, though she tried desperately to hold it back, as though it were improper to show it in front of a stranger. He didn't say anything until she had unfolded her arms and pushed her plate away. He rolled up his napkin and set it on the sandwich, though he was still hungry.

"I'm sorry," Stanton said.

She shook her head. "You can't imagine the pain that first day after. The first day without him there."

He nodded slowly. "Yes, I can."

They held each other's gaze for a moment, the moment broken only by the sound of her phone buzzing. She checked it and said, "I got the list from Greg. We'll have to do it in the morning. But where do you wanna start?"

"At the top and go down. I want to speak to all of them."

19

The list Katie had been emailed consisted of four names: all white men in their mid to late forties, three living on either unemployment or disability. Two lived with their parents, one was in prison, and one in a halfway house, newly released from the Washington State Penitentiary. As they drove the next morning, Stanton stared at the names on Katie's phone, wondering if the name itself could give him anything. But it couldn't. They were just words.

"What's the first guy's name?" she asked.

"Kyle Snell. Lives with his parents. He was convicted of distribution of child pornography in '89 and served a seventeen-year stint in a federal penitentiary in Colorado. Moved back here afterwards to be with his parents."

She glanced at him. "You seem like you know these types of guys pretty well. That couldn't have come just from a few years in a Sex Crimes unit."

"I have a PhD in psychology. Part of my research for the doctorate was in aberrant sexual behavior. I got to know men like Kyle Snell really well when I spent time with them. They don't talk to cops the same way they talk to researchers. They open up more. They don't understand why they do it either, and they think maybe the researcher can tell them."

"Could you?"

He shook his head. "No, there's no explanation. Albert Fish, a serial killer in the early twentieth century, used to purposely get in trouble at the age of two so that his mother would beat him. He couldn't achieve erection at that age, but the masochistic pleasure was there. Children don't even really have long-term memory at two, much less abnormal sexual desires. It's something else. Something inexplicable."

She was silent for a second. "I get the feeling being married to you wouldn't be easy. Normal cops don't know stuff like that."

He grinned. "You'll have to ask my ex-wife and my ex-fiancée how it was. I'm guessing you're right."

The building was a tall cylindrical skyrise surrounded by buildings that could've been on any corner in any upscale neighborhood in the country—the neighborhoods where people weren't frightened walking down the street at night. Katie parked, and they went to the front door, which was locked. Katie checked her phone for the apartment number and then dialed up.

"Yes?" a female voice said.

"This is Detective Katherine Wong with the Seattle Police Department. We need to speak with Kyle Snell."

A long pause. "I'm sorry, he isn't here."

"Ma'am, if I come up there and he's there, it's just going to cause more trouble for him and for you. Not less. We just want to talk. That's all."

Another pause. Stanton realized the woman was putting her hand over the speaker and talking with someone, the muffled tones barely audible. "Okay, hang on," she said.

A buzzer sounded, and Katie opened the door and held it for him. Stanton walked through and pressed the button for the elevator. Katie checked the surroundings, her eyes going from the expensive rug on the floor to the white leather couch in the corner.

They stepped into the elevator and headed to the tenth floor. Stanton had brought his firearm, and he hoped Katie wouldn't ask him to remove it and put it back in the car. He was a civilian here, after all. He had no authority to carry a concealed firearm in this state. It wouldn't look good if he had to actually use the weapon.

The tenth floor was as plush as the lobby, clean white carpets and glass looking down at the city, abstract paintings on the walls. Stanton walked a few paces behind Katie. He wanted to make certain she felt she was running the show.

She knocked on the door and an older woman wearing white pants and a beige sweater answered. The gold watch on her wrist gleamed in the sunlight. The woman looked from one detective to the other and said, "Yes?"

"We're here to speak with Kyle."

"I told you, he isn't here."

"May we have a look around?" Katie said.

The woman swallowed. "I don't see why I should allow that. I haven't done anything and I don't see a search warrant."

"If I have to get a—"

Stanton stepped forward. "We can talk out here in the hall. We don't care what's in his room."

The woman hesitated. "Wait here."

Katie looked at him, and he knew they both understood that the reason Kyle didn't want them to go in was because he had something in his room not allowed while he was on parole. It could have been pot or booze, pornography, or another felon or sex offender. Stanton didn't care about it, but from the look on Katie's face, she did. She hadn't learned yet that you had to pick your battles, and that if you tried to make a bust on every crime you saw, you would burn yourself out. Stanton, for the first time, realized how new Katie was at this.

Before he could say anything, a man was at the door. He was frail, thin to the point of looking unhealthy. He wore glasses, and his shirt was tucked into his jeans. He shut the door behind him and said, "I'm Kyle."

"Kyle Snell?" Katie said.

"Yes."

"We need to ask you a few questions about Reginald Carter."

He shook his head. "Never heard of him."

"He was in the news about a week ago."

Kyle's eyes went wide. "That guy who killed those girls? I didn't have nothing to do with that."

"We're not saying you did," Katie quickly said. "But we think you might know something about him or someone else he was working with."

"No, I don't know nothing about that. That shit with me was a long time ago. I was a different person then."

"You can never step into the same river twice," Stanton said.

Kyle responded, "Because the second time it's not the same river, and it's not the same man."

The mantra was frequently used in sex offender therapy.

"You're not in any trouble, Kyle," he said. "We just want to know about Reginald Carter. You were a hub at the time he was killing those girls. I think he watched child pornography, too. We didn't find a computer, but I'm betting whoever helped him kill those girls has it. Someone that you might've sent pornography to."

Kyle bit his lower lip and looked down at the floor. He was clearly debating what he could and couldn't tell them. "I don't do that anymore," Kyle said. "I've been in recovery since I got locked up."

"But I bet you still have those lists," Stanton said. "The police never take every computer. I just want the lists."

He swallowed. "If my PO knew I had a computer he didn't know about, I'd be back in prison. So I don't have one."

Stanton took a step closer. "You love children."

"No," Kyle snapped. "No, I don't. Not anymore."

"Yes you do. I know you do. I can see it in your eyes. The eyes don't lie, Kyle. When I mentioned children, your eyes lit up. That'll never go away, no matter how long you're in recovery. I know you love them, I know you believe you were helping them. Taking care of them. But this man we're looking for, he doesn't love children. He hates them. He ties them up in a dark basement and tortures them."

Kyle began to weep.

"Help me find him."

Kyle wiped his tears away. "I would never hurt a child. Ever. I do love them. They're gifts to us."

"So help me find him."

He wiped the rest of his tears away with his fingertips and nodded.

20

Kyle sat in the back of Katie's car as they drove farther downtown. Stanton hadn't asked, but he had no doubt that Kyle, like many sex offenders, had a residence his parole officer knew nothing about: somewhere to stash everything he wasn't supposed to have, rented under a fake name, and paid for with cash every month.

"Right here," Kyle said.

The apartment building was four stories and looked at least two decades too old to still be standing. The bricks were chipping off, the glass on the entryway was cracked, and the front lawn overflowed with weeds.

"I don't want you coming with me," Kyle said.

"That's fine."

He got out of the car, looked both ways, and then headed into the building, which had a keycode entry. From the car, Stanton could see his fingers move over the keypad. A four-digit combination: 4121. Kyle disappeared inside.

"How'd you know he'd do that?" Katie asked.

"Pedophiles—not the sadists, but the garden-variety pedophiles—think they're helping children. They think they're in love with them. Usually, the ones who torture and kill children are outcasts. A hub is typically not a sadist. That's not why he's doing what he's doing."

Katie looked into the apartment building. "You don't think we should go with him?"

"No. He's got things in there that will send him back to prison."

She tapped her fingers against the wheel. At any time, she could call this thing off, send Stanton packing, and arrest Kyle. If there had been a second man who'd helped Carter kidnap and kill those girls, he would get away.

"Katie, I don't know how long you've been in Homicide, but I've been in it longer. If you want to last, you have to prioritize. You can't go after everybody."

"You've never been a detective here, so don't patronize me. We don't let pedophiles keeping child porn in secret apartments slide."

"You have to. As odd as it is, that's the way this is gonna work. You have to go after the biggest fish you can, and always use the little fish."

She turned away, keeping her gaze fixed on another apartment building across the street. Stanton wondered what to say but wasn't sure exactly what the issue was. Pissing contests between agencies were common, but he suspected that's not what this was. Something else was going on. He knew women detectives had a rough time in a predominantly male-dominated field. Perhaps she'd been told what to do so much by men who knew less than she did that she'd developed a defense against it.

"I'm sorry," Stanton said. "I'm overstepping my bounds. I just need to know what happened to her. It's the not-knowing that eats you up. That's what you think about at night, and you picture all the horrible things that could've happened. I can't move on from it. Every relationship I have, my career, my dreams, it's all tied to this. I've never moved on. I didn't heal."

She exhaled and turned toward him. "You have more of a right to be here than I do. But there have to be some ground rules. I'm not comfortable with this. We can't do this again. If we're talking to somebody and he admits to a crime, we need to act on that information. Especially if it's a felony or a parole violation."

Stanton nodded. "Okay. It's your investigation. I'm just here to help if I can."

Kyle came back out a moment later. He had a scrap of white lined paper in his hand and got into the backseat. He handed it to Stanton. It was a list of names, at least seventy, maybe eighty. Stanton quickly scanned the paper and said, "Do you have addresses or phone numbers?"

"Sorry, man. Just emails and names. You can track down the addresses if you have a tech that knows what they're doing. Just a matter of getting everything from the email provider and the ISPs."

"I appreciate this. You did the right thing."

"Yeah," he said, leaning back into the seats, "let's just see if the dudes whose names I just gave you agree."

After dropping Kyle off, Stanton went back to his hotel room. Katie had been called to a scene, a murder-suicide of a married couple in Glitter Lake. She promised to call him tomorrow and that they would hit the other three names on the list Greg had given them.

Stanton had taken a photo of Kyle's list, and he counted the names once he was up in his room. Seventy-three names. Too many for him to interview in person. He called over to the Records Division in Honolulu and got the familiar voice of Amanda Nalathu. After exchanging greetings and getting an update on the weather in Honolulu, he asked if she could run background histories for seventy-three names.

"That many?"

"Yeah. I especially need lists of known acquaintances."

"All right, hon. Might take me a while, though."

Law enforcement databases across the country varied, based mostly on the fact that mayors of various cities could be bought by the database software companies, but one database in use in a lot of places was Spillman. A Spillman search would give Stanton almost everything he needed to know about these men. On top of that, Honolulu did extensive background searches that included financial information, aliases, known acquaintances, credit reports, and a list of known addresses. If Stanton needed to find a link between two people who had criminal histories, the search would give it to him. He had once found out that the suspect in a murder and the husband of the victim had shared a cell together for a few weeks, one for a drug charge and one for a DUI. It led to the arrest of the husband on aggravated murder charges to which he pled out on second-degree murder, with a sentence of life with possible parole.

Stanton ate at the grill downstairs and then watched television for a few hours before taking a nap. When he woke, evening was falling, and the sky darkened. Here, Stanton actually preferred the night. The grayness dulled his mind, but the night could've been night anywhere.

He pretended he was back on his beach on the island, surrounded by crystal-blue ocean. It helped calm him and lift the malaise that had settled in the past two days.

It suddenly dawned on him that he hadn't checked on Hanny. Knowing that Hanny was okay was suddenly important to him.

Stanton quickly showered and changed his shirt, though he wore the same pants and leather jacket. He headed down to the computer lounge and onto one of the old PCs they had for guests. After he input his room number, the computer booted up, and he logged into the dog care website. A color image came to life, about a dozen dogs in large kennels with blankets. Hanny was right in the center, lying on his paws, his eyes lazily drifting between the workers darting back and forth.

Stanton watched the dog for a few minutes and then rose and headed outside.

21

The city seemed to be waking up. When he'd lived here, Stanton had been too young to remember that Seattle catered more to the youth than anyone else. Bars, clubs, restaurants and lounges, jazz clubs, concerts, and coffee shops with poetry slams seemed to permeate the city once the sun fell. From his youth, he only remembered a city that was wet and quiet. A new vibrancy had settled there, and he guessed the city had easily tripled in population since he'd lived there, spreading much more widely over the valleys and hills.

He walked briskly down the street, enjoying the salty air, and headed toward the ocean like a scrap of metal flung toward a magnet. Even if he couldn't be in the ocean, he could be near it.

The beach had its own restaurant right there, catering to seafood enthusiasts. Stanton asked for a table outside and stared out over the sea, a distant ship's lights twinkling red and white toward shore.

"Can I get you something to drink?" the waitress said. "A vodka tonic or a beer?"

"Just an orange juice would be great."

She nodded and headed back to the kitchen. She was pretty; blonde and skinny with large white teeth and blue eyes. Stanton watched as she walked away. The acute pain of loneliness hit him just then, the feeling that no one in the world would really care much if he weren't in it anymore. Much of the time, he knew, those thoughts could take over if he didn't pay attention. Depression had plagued him his entire life. His faith alleviated the pain but never abolished it. It was always there like some wound that wouldn't heal.

A text came to his phone on the table. It was from Katie, and read, *You doing okay?*

Surviving, he replied.

I'll be here a couple more hours if you wanna grab a late dinner later

He hesitated before replying. Maybe she wanted someone to have dinner with and it didn't really matter who, or she felt sorry for him because he was here alone. Of course, it was always possible she was interested in him, but he decided he didn't have enough information to decide. He was interested in her; he knew that, at least. She had an odd kind of strength, as though she displayed courage and tenacity, but inside was insecure, a chaotic mess that couldn't be organized. Though physically attractive, Stanton didn't think that's what drew him to her.

Late dinner sounds great.

When the waitress came back out, Stanton told her he wouldn't be eating and asked for the orange juice to go. He was in the middle of paying when another text came in. This one was from Amanda, letting him know the reports were emailed.

Stanton quickly paid and headed back to the hotel.

He logged into one of the hotel's computers and then tried to access the Honolulu PD server to get to his email. His access was denied. He sighed and stared at the screen, debating what to do. Without access to his resources in Honolulu, he was completely reliant on Katie—not a position he liked being in. But he couldn't see that there was anything else he could do. Sending confidential information in unsecured email was illegal, and Amanda could get fired. He couldn't do that to her.

He decided when he met Katie for dinner tonight he would ask her for thorough background checks. Then he stopped, wondering if they would ever know if he just sent them to a private email address, and then deleted the account. Amanda would be at risk, but what choice did he have?

Think you can send them to a private email? he wrote to Amanda.

Against policy, sorry.

I know. But I'm stuck and don't have anywhere else to go. The guy I'm looking for hurts kids.

It seemed as though a full minute passed before the reply came.

Okay.

Stanton quickly created a new email address on Gmail and sent it to Amanda. He'd close the account after he got the list.

A slight twinge of guilt came with the elation that he would have a list of active child pornography addicts who lived near where his sister had disappeared. Though a lot of research had shown that offenders who only consumed child pornography and didn't have a history of physical abuse against children likely wouldn't harm children, he felt the research was flawed. He'd seen it in traditional pornography addicts. They would build a tolerance to the pornography, their brains adjusting in much the same way a cocaine addict adjusts to the levels of cocaine consumption. They would become involved in more deviant pornography, until finally they discovered rape fantasy and child pornography. Eventually, those would grow dull as well, and they would have to move on to more stimulation, whether flashing, masturbating in public, or full-on sexual assault.

The problem with the research was that research could only be conducted on those offenders who had been caught. Only the most out-of-control offenders were caught—the ones who couldn't be patient and plan. The ones who could wait and think about how to fulfill their addiction covered their tracks well and were difficult to find and study.

The email came through. He opened it and quickly flipped through it. Seventy-three names. He excluded the ones who lived more than a hundred miles from Rosebud and was left with a list of forty-one offenders in the Seattle area. He would collect a list just like this from all four names Greg had given them and then would have to whittle it down until he had someone that fit the criteria.

It was a long shot. If Carter did have a partner, anything could've happened in twenty-seven years. He could be dead, he could be in prison, he could've moved… The likelihood that Stanton would find him was nearly zero.

Stanton saved the background checks on the hotel's computer and then emailed them to himself before deleting them from the computer. He walked outside, reading the names on the list, their financial histories, their addresses and known acquaintances. It wouldn't be as simple as seeing Carter's name as someone's acquaintance. Carter was a respected teacher and leader in his church. He wouldn't have associated with men who had criminal histories. This would be an association that was completely in private.

Stanton got another text from Katie saying she was done and that there was a great steak place near her condo. Stanton got the address. He checked the clock on his phone and saw that he'd been walking for more than twenty minutes. He hurried back to his car and began the drive over to the restaurant.

22

On the way over, the only thing Stanton could think about was talking to the other three names on Greg's list. Kyle had already given them so much, if they could get anywhere near as much information from the other three, he had no doubt they would find someone who knew something about Reginald Carter.

The restaurant had a sloped, curving roof that looked like something on a Buddhist temple rather than a steak house. He parked and stepped out of the car, glancing up at the moon, which was peeking out from behind gray-black clouds.

Inside, the restaurant was packed, primarily with families. He saw Katie sitting at a booth, gazing at her phone, and he headed over. He sat down across from her, and she put the phone down and smiled at him.

"Sorry for making you wait," he said.

"No worries. What were you doing?"

"Some follow-up to the list Kyle gave us. I've narrowed it down to forty-one names that lived within a hundred miles of Rosebud, and six names that live less than twenty miles away."

"You wanna interview them all?"

He shrugged. "I don't know. Usually I have a goal in an investigation, something concrete. I don't have that here. It feels like I just want some sort of forward motion just to be doing something."

The waiter interrupted them and took their order. Katie wanted a steak and Stanton asked for a salad. When he left, Katie said, "At some point, no forward motion'll be possible. What then?"

"I don't know. Go back home, I guess."

She hesitated. "When Brian passed, I did everything I could to find out why that woman was on the road. I was obsessed with it. It… consumed everything else. My marriage fell apart, we sold the house and everything else. I had to take almost a year away from the force. The obsession ate me alive. I can see some of that in you. Don't let it take over."

Stanton rested his hands on the table, feeling the cracks and crevices of the wood. "It already has. I had no business becoming a police officer. I shouldn't have divorced my first wife, or broken up with my fiancée later. I shouldn't be thirty-seven years old and living by myself. I can see where it began, though, as clearly as anything: the moment I found out my sister was gone, I knew she was dead. I don't know how. But I just knew. And from that moment I wasn't the same person. How can I not be obsessed?"

She shook her head. "I don't know, but you have to. Otherwise there'll be nothing left."

Water arrived, and Stanton took a sip. They spoke of other, more pleasant things: Katie's hobby of bird watching—something Stanton thought only biologists and retirees did—her love of movies, and why she had chosen to become a police officer. Stanton talked about his sons and about the rejuvenation that living on a tropical island brought him every day.

"You seem like the most unlikely cop I've ever met," she said.

She had said it offhandedly, not meaning anything by it—in fact,

Stanton suspected it was meant as a compliment—but it stung him. He shouldn't have been a police officer. Being a cop was being part of a gun culture, machismo, and bragging about machismo. It was why people left the military and joined police agencies right after. The transition would be seamless for someone who understood the culture. A culture he never fit into.

"I better go," she said as they finished up. "I'm on call, and I wanna get a couple of hours' sleep first."

Stanton picked up the check, and they left together. He walked her to her car and there was a moment, just a moment, where it seemed as though something was between them—just enough that if he gave her a kiss, it wouldn't be entirely awkward. Still, when it came to these things, his instincts weren't the best, so he decided to play it safe. He leaned in and pecked her on the cheek, and she grinned.

As she drove away, Stanton stood in the parking lot and watched her taillights. He should sleep, too, so he could give everything he had the next few days and then head home. But he knew that wasn't where the case was going. There was no other home for him. No matter where he was, he was still here, chasing down the ghost of a girl who loved him unconditionally when no one else did.

He pulled out the list of the six men receiving child pornography from Kyle, the ones who lived near Carter, and decided he wouldn't be sleeping just yet.

23

The first home was a nondescript rambler with a white pickup in the driveway. Stanton parked across the street. The typical lower-class neighborhood seemed clean and quiet for this time of night, other than a Mustang filled with teenagers that sped by on the road, blaring metal. Stanton waited until the neighborhood was quiet again before getting out of his car.

A breeze blew, and the air sent a chill up his back. He flipped up the collar of his jacket. He had a quick look inside the pickup and saw empty beer cans tucked under the passenger seat. Stanton went to the front door of the house and listened; a television was on.

He knocked and waited and then knocked again. Before long, a man in overalls with a thick, gray beard came to the door. His glasses were so large they were almost comical, and even though Stanton could see the man was just watching television, he wore a baseball cap and boots.

"Yeah?" the man said.

"Are you Devin?"

"Yeah."

"Devin, I'd like to speak with you for a minute if that's okay."

The man eyed him a second. "'Bout what?"

"About the child porn you have on your computer."

The man's face dropped, his skin instantly turning pale. Or at least, that was Stanton's impression—the light from inside the home and the darkness outside cast shadows across the man's face.

"You need to leave my property."

"If I leave, my next call is to Seattle PD. Or you could give me ten minutes of your time."

Devin shifted his weight from foot to foot like a child who needed to pee. Stanton realized he didn't know he was doing it.

"Come in," he finally said.

Stanton shut the door behind him. The home looked as if a hurricane had been through it. Fast-food bags, empty milk cartons, beer cans, boxes of wine and pizza littered the living room like a rug. The odor was somewhere between wet dog and rotting food.

Stanton couldn't see a way to get to the couch without stepping in garbage, so he stood by the door.

"So?" Devin said.

"You were on an email list. The list was run by someone with the name PCTPMaster. You know the list I'm talking about?"

The man began rocking again and had to sit down. He wrung his hands together. "I ain't goin' back inside. I did me twenty-three years outta fifty-six years of life inside. I ain't goin' back no matter what."

"I'm not here to arrest you. I'm not even a cop in this state. I'm from Hawaii. I'm here because of a case from a long time ago, a young girl who may have been one of Reginald Carter's victims. Do you know about Carter?"

"Yeah, I seen it on the news. They talked 'bout it damn near every day for a week."

Stanton nodded. "I'm just looking for people who knew Carter.

Did you ever have any interaction with him?"

"No, man. No. I ain't like that. I keep to myself. I got my disability checks every month, I jerk off every morning and before bed, and that's it. That's my life."

"And that's enough?"

"Shit. 'Enough' is sometimes all you got."

Stanton glanced around the home. "I don't suppose if I asked you where you were on a particular day you would remember."

The man looked at him a moment, and then laughed. "Shit, I don't know where I was yesterday. It's that medication they got me on. The ah… what you call it? Serakin."

"That's a powerful drug."

"Schizophrenia," he said, nodding. "Doctor inside told me it's genetic, and I told him no one in my family ever had it. Not a one." He began rocking again. "My daddy used to do things to me. That's where it come from. I was just a kid before then."

"Do you know anyone else on that list?" Stanton said, trying to keep him focused. "Anyone who ever mentioned Carter or someone who was hurting young girls?"

He shook his head. "No, man. I keep to myself. I see my mama and that's about it. Go out for groceries sometimes. I don't know no one."

Stanton knew one of the effects of Serakin was the inability to form emotional connections. Serakin was a powerful antipsychotic that left its users dulled. He doubted Devin would be much of a liar or have any friends or even acquaintances, given its side effects. In some ways, it mimicked a lobotomy.

"Thanks for your time."

Stanton left the home and shut the door before sitting down on the porch. He stared up at the stars. This seemed like an impossible feat. He had to visit all these men and try to find out where they were on a single night twenty-seven years ago and whether they knew a dead man accused of serial murder. No one would admit to it. There had to be something else, some other link in Carter's life that he was overlooking.

He paused, holding his breath, and then released it slowly through his nose. He waited a minute then rose and poked his head into the home again. Devin hadn't gotten off the couch. Something on the television had caught his attention, and he was transfixed.

"Devin... Devin, could you look at me please?"

"Yeah, man. Yeah."

"I know you weren't heavily involved in the community, but were there others who were? A group that met at someone's house or something like that?"

Stanton had learned that the child pornography and pedophile communities were tightly knit, routinely swapping video files and actual children. Adoption was the preferred method of acquiring victims, but nephews and nieces and the children of neighbors were more readily at hand. Pedophiles had no sense of familial bonds; their own children or grandchildren were victims in their eyes as much as strangers. Stanton had even had a case of a father who passed around his eight-year-old daughter to more than twenty men in his group. When Stanton found him, the man had put a bullet in his head, choosing to die rather than live a life in prison being raped and passed around the same way he had raped and passed around his daughter.

"A group?" Devin said.

"Yeah, a group. People who got together and talked about how much they loved kids. Shared videos and tips. Things like that."

"I guess. I was invited to that bar down there in Clearfield a few times. Never went, though." Devin's rocking had reached feverish proportions. The questions were bringing up memories that were stimulating him too much.

"What bar?" Stanton said.

"Trap's. Or Rap's. Somethin' like that." He rubbed his beard. "You need to leave now."

Stanton nodded. "I will. But first I need you to make sure. Is it Rap's or Trap's?"

"Trap's. It was Trap's."

"Okay, thanks."

Stanton shut the door. He googled Trap's in Clearfield, Washington, and got a hit. No website, but there was an address and a map listing. He hurried to his Jeep, glanced back once at Devin's home, and sped away.

24

Trap's looked just as Stanton thought it would. Twenty stone steps or more led below to the basement level of a two-story building. The building housed a sports supply store and a retailer that sold four-wheelers and Jet Skis. Stanton parked away from the other cars and watched, hoping to observe some of the people going in and out, but no one did. So he left his Jeep and headed down the stairs.

The interior of the bar was as dark as he had ever seen in a public place—no windows, not that that would help, but not even any attempts at extra lighting. A few lights at the entrance, and a few at the back leading to the bathrooms, and darkness in between. Each table was so dimly lit that Stanton could barely make out the faces of the few men who were there. Trap's wasn't a place to mingle away the hours; it was a place to get away from the eyes of everyone else.

In the back of the large space was an oval bar, and Stanton went over and sat down on the end. The bartender wore a green polo shirt and had a mustache so thick it covered his upper lip. He didn't pay any attention to Stanton.

A man came up to him then from the darkness. Thin and with a multicolored baseball cap turned to the side, he sat down next to Stanton. He had an unlit cigarette dangling from his mouth. "Ain't seen you here."

"No."

"You a cop?"

Stanton looked at him. "No, just… lonely, I guess."

"No shit. Name's Stewart."

"Nice to meet you."

Stewart whistled to the bartender and said, "Two beers, Jack." He turned to Stanton. "So what can we do so you ain't so lonely?"

"I don't know. What do you have?"

The man grinned and dipped into his pocket. He came out with several types of pills. "Whatever you want. Downers, uppers, mescaline, 'ludes, whatever."

Stanton pulled out his wallet and laid a hundred on the bar. "Whatever that will buy me in Quaaludes. For now."

Stewart nodded and laid two pills on the bar before taking the bill and shoving it into the same pocket the pills had been in.

"You need anything else, you ask me," Stewart said, rising.

"Actually, these will help, but there's other ways to alleviate loneliness."

Stewart grinned again. "You like cock or pussy?"

Stanton took the two pills off the bar and held them in his palm while the bartender placed two mugs of beer in front them. "Doesn't matter, as long as it's… not too old."

Stewart chuckled. He took one of the beers and drank it down in a matter of seconds. "Can't help you there. Sorry, compadre." He began walking away.

"Wait," Stanton said. "Maybe you can't help, but I bet you know someone who can."

Stewart waved his cigarette up and down using his lips. "Ask Jack."

With that, the man disappeared again into the darkness, an apparition that came out only to serve its purpose and then climbed into the darkness again. Stanton turned toward the bartender, Jack. The man had heard the exchange but hadn't made a move to come over to Stanton. He was cautious, and Stanton couldn't simply ask for information and get it. There would be another way.

Stanton pretended to nurse his beer, but he just gazed into the glass. The dim lighting brought out sparkles of gold. Froth seeped over the lip, and he set it on a napkin and watched intently as the froth dripped down.

An hour passed, and he didn't move. Not until Jack said something to another bartender and headed toward the bathrooms. Stanton rose and followed him.

As he passed the booths and the tables, he could see the hard, unkind faces of the men who had gathered there. Some of them grinned at Stanton, and some of them just stared with eyes glazed over like marbles, alcohol and apathy slowly killing their souls.

The men's bathroom was off to the right down a small hallway. Stanton stepped through the door and saw Jack at the urinal. Stanton went to the far end, urinated, and then went to the sink to wash his hands as Jack did the same.

"Hi," Stanton said.

"Hello," Jack said, not taking his eyes off his own face in the mirror.

"This is my first time here. I like how quiet it is."

Jack turned the water off and grabbed a paper towel. "I figured that."

"I was told you were the man to see, though."

"See about what?"

"About anything I might need."

Jack turned to him, his hands in his pockets as he stared into his eyes. "You didn't drink your beer. You sat there for over an hour and didn't touch it."

"I don't like mixing alcohol and 'ludes."

Jack nodded. "What is it you think I can do for you?"

He shrugged. "I was just feeling lonely tonight."

Jack lightly bit his lower lip, his eyes never leaving Stanton's. His barrier wasn't going down.

"Forget it. Sorry I bothered you." Stanton began walking toward the exit, his heart beating a million miles a minute as he grabbed the door handle. If Jack didn't stop him, this was it. He would have to leave.

"Hold on," Jack said from behind him. "Come back around closing at two."

Stanton held the door open as Jack walked out and back to the bar. He checked the clock on his iPhone; he still had another three hours. He left the bar, threw the pills into the nearest trash, and got into his Jeep.

25

Stanton drove down to Puget Sound, a massive connection of waterways and basins, all coming from and leading to the Pacific Ocean. In his youth, his family used to rent a cabin nearby. One morning when Stanton was maybe nine, he left the cabin before anyone else woke up, and he headed out to the beach. A canoe was lashed to a pier, and he got in just as he heard footfalls behind him. He turned to see Elizabeth hurrying across the rocky beach.

"You're not going out alone," she said, jumping into the canoe.

"I'm fine," he insisted.

She lay back, crossing one leg over another. "Start paddling, 'cause I'm not doing it."

Stanton grunted futilely and then picked up an oar. Untying from the pier, he paddled through the choppy greenish-blue water until they were far from shore and drifting out in the open. Lush forests covered the distant shoreline, interspersed with homes and cabins. In this particular section of Puget Sound, an inlet led directly out to the Pacific, and Stanton tried paddling there.

"You won't make it," Elizabeth said.

"I can try."

"What was that?" she gasped.

"What?" he said, not stopping.

"Stop paddling, Jon."

He stopped, and set the paddle down. He couldn't hear anything but the water and, somewhere off in the distance, a bird of some sort.

Then he heard it.

The mournful cry, low at first. Then building up in a crescendo of sound until it ended in almost human sounding clicks: a whale.

"Oh my gosh, oh my gosh, oh—"

"They're not sharks," Stanton said. "They're not going to hurt us."

Elizabeth gripped the sides of the canoe until her knuckles turned white. Stanton scanned the water around them but couldn't see anything. They sat out there a long time, hoping to see or hear the whale again, but they never did.

As Stanton parked the Jeep near shore, he thought about that memory and wondered if, of the three of them who shared that experience, he was the only one that was still alive.

The moon had come out of hiding, and the clouds dissipated enough to fully illuminate the water in a soft white glow. Stanton sat down on a log past the tree line, watching the waves as they rolled in, bringing with them bits of driftwood and debris. Puget Sound wasn't as clean as he remembered as a child. Several companies dumped waste into it, and he knew there had been a major problem of killer whale deaths from the toxicity of the water. Still, right now, with the moon shining over it, the water was beautiful.

His phone buzzed. It was Katie.

"Hey," he said.

"Sorry to bug you. Just checking in about our game plan for tomorrow. I've cleared it with Thomas, and he's going to be helping us. I'm going to try to get a few uniformed officers to run down names on the list, too."

"That's great."

"Is something wrong?"

"No, why?"

"I thought you'd be more excited. We're going to have help."

Stanton stared down at the rocks by his feet. If she knew what he was doing tonight, she would cut off her help and maybe even charge him with a crime. "I'm just tired," he lied. "Can I call you tomorrow?"

"Sure," she said. She sounded disappointed, as though she'd wanted something else from him.

"You okay?"

"Fine. That sounds great. Just call me tomorrow."

Stanton hung up and stared at his phone for a few seconds before putting it away and turning his gaze back out to the water. Perhaps she wanted him to ask if he could come over tonight. Katie had loneliness in her eyes that seemed to dissipate the more they talked. He recognized it because he had the same loneliness.

Stanton lay back. Several small rocks and pebbles made it less comfortable than it could've been, but he ignored the discomfort and stared at the moon before closing his eyes and disappearing.

When Stanton woke, it wasn't of his own volition. He heard something farther off in the forest, the broken rhythm of an animal dashing through vegetation. Stanton sat up and then he got to his feet before scanning the forest around him. He decided he didn't need to know what animal had shown interest in him and instead got to his

Jeep and went back to the bar.

The interior had less smoke and fewer people. Jack was at the bar. He mumbled something to the other bartender and then sat down in a booth and motioned for Stanton to sit with him. His gut in knots, Stanton complied.

"How did you hear about this place?" he asked.

"Devin told me."

"Devin doesn't talk to nobody."

Stanton leaned back in the seat, striking a more casual pose. "I'm his nurse. Or at least the nurse his mother hired. He doesn't like me taking care of him so I just check up on him. Make sure he's eating, stuff like that. He told me about a group I might be interested in when we discussed some of our mutual preferences. I'm Jon, by the way."

He nodded. "What exactly do you need, Jon?"

"Girls. Young, but not too young. Thirteen to fifteen. I'm not a pervert."

"Nobody said you are. It's perfectly natural, what you feel. Society likes to pretend it isn't, but they'll come around. Look at the gays. Thirty years ago, they were outcasts. Now you're the outcast if you don't think two dudes should be able to get married. We can do the same thing, reclaim our image. Get the lobbying in place, the money. We already have the organizing power. First thing is the name. We gotta call ourselves 'pedosexuals,' not 'pedophiles.' That name's been ruined. Once pedosexuals sticks, we can start with the lobbying. Shit, I may not live to see it, but it'll happen. You just watch." He pulled out a package of cigarettes but didn't do anything with them. "Do you have any special tastes?"

"Like what?"

He shrugged. "Are you going to be rough, or do you like it soft and gentle?"

Stanton had to physically swallow to keep his anger and revulsion in check. The way Jack spoke about the rape of a child was so casual, he could've been talking about the latest baseball scores or traffic on his way in to work. It held no disgust for Jack.

"I sometimes… get violent."

He nodded and lit a cigarette, pulling an ashtray across the table to him. "I can't promise race. White girls are the hardest to get and cost the most. Blacks are easier to get and cost less. There's always Asians, too, and we can talk about cost based on how used up they are. Mexicans are harder to get up here."

"How much are we talking about?"

"One night? Two thousand. A weekend is five. If you want someone you can keep for longer, that's got to be negotiated."

"How do you get the girls?"

"You don't need to know that."

Stanton nodded, glancing to the red tip of the cigarette. "No, I guess I don't. When does this happen?"

"When do you need her by?"

"Soon as possible, I guess."

"Give me your information, and I'll get back to you."

With that, Jack rose and went back to cleaning up the rest of the bar. Stanton sat there a moment, unsure exactly what had just happened, and then went to the bar and wrote his cell number and name on a napkin. He handed it to the other bartender and said,

"Would you give that to Jack, please?"

"Sure," the man said.

Stanton glanced at Jack, who was busy pulling the vacuum out of a utility closet, but Jack didn't notice him anymore.

Outside, the air seemed cool as Stanton strolled back to his Jeep. He kept his head low, staring at his feet—a habit he'd picked up as a kid that he sometimes reverted to. Just as he neared the Jeep and looked up, a figure rushed at him from the shadows.

It was too close for Stanton to react. The figure slammed into him, knocking the wind out of him as he toppled over. Stanton wrapped his arms around the dark shadow and felt ribs, a man who writhed and fought on top of him. Another man ran out from behind a car. Stanton reached for his gun, but the man on top of him grabbed his arm. Stanton placed his knees against the man's ribs, squeezed, and then bit into his neck with everything he had. The man squealed just as the other one reached them.

Stanton pulled his gun free and pressed the weapon against the man's ribs. The man on top immediately jumped off and ran, shouting, "He's got a fucking gun!"

The other one stopped, unsure what to do, and Stanton jumped to his feet. He rushed the man, who turned to run but not quickly enough. Stanton tackled him like a linebacker, landing on top. He lifted his gun and rather than firing, he slammed the butt into the man's jaw, and then his nose. He kept bashing his face, cracking cheekbones and teeth.

"Stop!"

Stanton stopped, breathing heavily, and turned. Jack stood at the top of the stairs, his eyes wide. The man underneath Stanton pushed him away and got up. He stumbled over to the car he'd been hiding behind and held onto the trunk to support himself. A slick trail of blood dripped down over the car from the man's nose and mouth. His hand slipped, and he collapsed onto the pavement, taking deep, gurgled breaths.

"He needs a hospital," Jack said.

Rage built inside Stanton, pure anger and disgust, like a ball of fire in his gut that was burning its way out. He held his Desert Eagle low and ran up to Jack, pressed the muzzle against his temple, his eyes gazing into Jack's.

"I will kill you," Stanton spat. "Do you believe me?"

Jack, frozen with terror, managed only a small nod.

"Reginald Carter. Do you know who he is?"

Jack nodded again.

Stanton gripped his collar, holding him in place. "He had a partner, someone helping him. I want to know who he is."

Jack swallowed. "I… I had them attack you because I thought you were lying. We were… going to see who you really were. Sometimes fathers of the kids come here, and they bring—"

"Shut up!" Stanton said, pushing the gun harder into his head. "Shut up now, or I swear I will kill you."

Jack swallowed again, his eyes closed now as though expecting the shot that would end his life. "I don't know anything. I just arrange the girls and screen the guys that come here. That's it."

"Where do you get the girls from?"

"Some guy."

Stanton swept Jack's legs out from under him. As soon as he hit the pavement, Stanton pushed his knee into the man's chest, and when he opened his mouth to exhale in pain, Stanton shoved the muzzle inside his mouth, pushing past the teeth. He couldn't control himself. There was no reason or sense left in him. The only thing he saw was Elizabeth's face in the canoe, gazing up at the sky, one leg dangling lazily over the other.

"Not good enough," Stanton said. "I want a name. Now." He cocked the gun.

"Tad. Lockwood." His words were muffled with the gun in his mouth.

"Tad Lockwood. You're sure?"

"I'm sure. I'm sure. I give him the money, and the kids show up at the guy's house. That's it. Someone goes and picks the girls up later. I don't know anything else."

Stanton, his heart pounding as though battery acid were pumping through it, eased the gun out of Jack's mouth but didn't holster it. He stared down at the man, who looked weak and pathetic. His eyes, once full of certainty and calm in the bar, were now filled with an utter terror at meeting a force greater than himself. After all was said and done, he was just a coward.

"You let them meet here?"

He nodded.

"Not anymore. If I find out there's one more meeting here, I'll be back for you. But I won't kill you. I'll let them stick you in the pen. You know what they do to *pedosexuals* in the pen?"

Jack nodded.

Stanton stood still. His mind was clearing now, his heart rate lowering to something resembling normal. He looked back at his two attackers. They were clearly unarmed, and he figured they probably would've held him down and checked his identification, verified he was who he said he was, maybe tried to frighten him a little. They weren't prepared for a fight where they could be killed. They were meant to scare him away.

As much as he wanted to, Stanton couldn't call the police. He'd committed more crimes here than anyone. If he called, he would be the one taken away in handcuffs. He would have to let Jack slide and hope that the threat that he would be back would be enough to deter him. That, and an anonymous tip to the Special Victims detectives at the Seattle PD.

Stanton got back into his Jeep, started it, and drove out of the parking lot. His eyes never turned toward Jack.

26

The next morning, Stanton woke up with a severe headache. He searched the bathroom in his hotel room and didn't find the ibuprofen he'd bought, so he dressed and went downstairs. The gift shop had various aids, and he bought some aspirin and a drink with caffeine before sitting down in a comfortable chair in the lobby.

The previous night was bits and pieces of a blur. All he remembered was barely controllable anger welling inside him. There wasn't a doubt in his mind that he would've killed Jack if the man hadn't given him what he wanted, and that frightened Stanton to no end. His father had once told him that the power of being a police officer would eventually corrupt him, corrupt anyone, but Stanton hadn't believed it at the time. Now he wondered if any amount of power eventually chipped away at that part of the psyche that held back the natural urges people felt, the urges that destroyed everything and everyone around them.

He called Honolulu PD for a Spillman check on Tad Lockwood of Washington. He got a hit on a Thaddeus J. Lockwood and asked that the report be emailed to him at the new Gmail account that he hadn't yet deleted. When Katie called and asked if he was ready to track down some names on the list they had, he told her he wasn't feeling well and needed to stay in the hotel today.

"Do you need anything?" she politely asked.

"No, just some sleep I think."

"Okay. Well, I'll give you a call if we turn up anything interesting."

Stanton felt bad for lying, but he had no choice. She wasn't prepared to go to the places he was going.

The report came halfway through his breakfast of cereal and fruit at a pancake house near the hotel. He didn't read it at first. The pancakes had gooey syrup with a hint of strawberry and maple and were the best things he'd eaten in a few days. He finished them entirely before polishing off the orange juice and paying.

After trying his son Mathew, he left a message saying, "Hey, Matty, it's your dad. I just... I just felt like talking to you and hearing your voice. Call me back if you get a minute." Stanton then leaned back in the booth and stared out the window.

The violent storm he was certain he'd heard last night had dissipated, leaving only a whirling mess of gray and dull white in the sky, a soup of thunderclouds. Every fifteen minutes or so, it would start to drizzle, the patter of raindrops ending their fall against cars, streets, and people echoing through his head. Stanton took it all in, the gray like a cloud over his soul. He felt physically and psychologically weaker, maybe even spiritually weaker, as if his blood had turned to slush, and his body had to work that much harder just to keep him alive. He rested his head against the cool glass, his eyes fixed on the pavement outside, the dark droplets spattering and disappearing.

After a good fifteen or twenty minutes, he opened the report from HPD and got Tad Lockwood's address.

Tad had a history of sex offenses and violence spanning decades, the most egregious of which was a forcible sodomy charge when he was sixteen. With his records sealed and no requirement to register as a sex offender since the incident happened when he was a minor, the system lost track of him for a good ten years before he turned up on an aggravated assault case. From then on, his history was a list of violence—primarily domestic violence, but never enough to rise to the level of landing him in prison.

Stanton rose and headed to his Jeep. The rain battered him, seemingly increasing in velocity based on his being outside. The drizzle turned into a downpour. Luckily the Jeep had a top, and he turned on the heater and sat quietly for a few moments, feeling the heat from the vents on the palms of his hands.

Tad lived in a section of Seattle known as Crown Hill. Stanton had been there a few times but didn't remember it well. He had to put the address into the GPS on his phone so he could find it.

Passing homes and businesses in this small community reminded him of Santa Monica: an insular section of a larger city completely cut off from the rest. It had its own atmosphere, its own sense of what made it unique and why. Stanton could see that in the people he passed. They shared some secret they didn't want to reveal to the rest of the world.

The Lockwood house looked like any other on this block: beige and brown, a small lawn with a driveway, and a flower patch near the porch. Stanton parked at the curb and hurried up to the door, the rain pounding down against the city to a deafening roar. He hit the door with the side of his fist and then rang the doorbell several times.

Stanton looked up at the house, staring into each window to see if someone was looking back, but no one was. He thought about leaving, but something told him to stay. Something he needed was here. He could feel it in his bones; sometimes instincts were all he had to go on.

He ran off the porch and around to the side door. He tried the knob, but the door was locked. Peering in through the window on the upper half of the door, he saw a hallway leading into a kitchen. A shoe rack was pressed against the wall with an assortment of old sneakers and sandals filling the slots. The parking area was just a metal sheet jutting out from the house, covering enough space for two vehicles. Stanton slipped under it, the sound of the rain even louder as it drummed onto the metal.

The backyard was large but completely unkempt. The grass was green but long enough to cover Stanton's shoes when he stepped into it. A few trees, a few bushes, and nothing else. The back door was locked as well. A basement window was next to the door, in a window well. Stanton hopped down there and tried the window. It slid open.

For a moment, he just listened to the rain and didn't go inside. He counted five breaths before he climbed inside, the rainwater washing down over his eyes and into his mouth, leaving a salty, slightly artificial taste. Hawaii's rain didn't taste like that. The islands hadn't developed enough industry to scar the skies.

The basement didn't have any furniture beyond a few slim mattresses laid out in front of a television. The light was on, but the house was completely silent. Stanton crossed the basement and peeked down a hallway, seeing a bathroom off to the right. He went in, took off his shirt, and dried himself with a towel before putting the shirt back on. Strands of hair hung down over his eyes, and he caught a glimpse of what he must've looked like at twenty, a beach-bum surfer who couldn't afford a haircut. He remembered himself then as enormously poor, and enormously happy. Possibly more than he ever had been in his life.

Going back into the room with the television, he scanned the space for any papers. Maybe some bills indicating who lived here. Spillman went off DMV and IRS addresses and sometimes wasn't up to date. The worst thing that could happen was that he could frighten some poor family half to death, crawling through their basement window, or maybe even get shot at.

The main room was bare. So were the two rooms that made up the rest of the basement. He found the stairs leading up to the rest of the house and waited at the bottom step. What was he doing here? Was he really here just on the off chance that Tad knew Reginald Carter? Maybe even supplied girls to him? It seemed tenuous at best. But what else did he have?

Slowly, he began climbing the steps.

27

Katie sat in her office staring at the names Kyle had gotten her and Stanton on the list in front of her: sex offenders who might possibly have known Reginald Carter. Of the two dozen calls she'd placed, ten of the names on the list belonged to men who had passed away, another nine were men who were serving out life sentences, and when she got in touch with the remainder, they told her they didn't know who Reginald Carter was. She would go out and interview them, get a sense of whether they were telling the truth or not, but this seemed like a daunting task, something she would have to devote herself to full time, or do it in her personal time. Neither of which she thought she could do.

Thomas walked in and sat on the couch. He crossed one leg over the other.

"What?" she said.

"What?"

"You have that smug grin on your face you get when you think you've done something clever."

"Well, maybe I have."

Katie leaned back in her chair. "What'd you do?"

"Oh, nothing big. Just solved the Richards homicide."

"How?"

"Got a confession from the neighbor across the street. Fucker was tough. Took me six hours. He kept asking to go to the bathroom, and I would tell him just a few more questions and then get into it with him again. He finally had to piss so bad he gave it up. They got into a fight over a girl they were both seeing. Richards clocked him and the neighbor pulled out his piece and put a cap in him."

Katie grinned. "I love when you think you're being hip."

"I am hip. And you're welcome for taking one of the red ones down off the board." He rose to head out and then stopped. He looked over the files on her desk. "You're not still chasing down that Carter thing, are you?"

"Yeah," she said with a sigh. "For all the good it'll do. There're too many people, and they all just tell me they didn't know him. Hard to prove someone knew someone else without having the time to dig through the person's life."

"Katie," he said, putting his hands in his pockets, "this case is closed. You gotta let it go."

"I will. I'm just following up a little for one of the victims."

"One of the victims, or Jon Stanton?"

"He is one of the victims."

"His sister wasn't at the house. Just a ring. For all we know, Carter found it at the school and took it home."

"I don't believe that and neither do you."

He shrugged. "Doesn't matter. It was almost thirty years ago. If there was any evidence, it's gone now."

She let out a deep breath and closed the files in front of her. "I don't know. I feel like there's something here. Just doesn't feel closed, in my gut. When we caught it, I thought it'd be simple, but there's some angle we're missing."

"My advice? Let it go. Let Jon Stanton get back on a plane to his little island and let the big boys get back to work."

"You really don't like him, do you?"

"I don't dislike him."

"Other than being perfectly polite, what did he do to you?"

Thomas waved his hand in the air, turning toward the photos on her wall. "Just his swagger."

"His swagger?"

"The way he spoke to me. I don't know. Like he was hot shit."

"I don't get that at all. It seemed like he was humble and just here because he's in a lot of pain."

"Yeah, well, a woman would think that."

"What's that supposed to mean?"

He turned toward her. "Nothing. Sorry. Listen, he's fine. But don't let him drag you into this thing. The case is off the board. Let sleeping dogs lie."

With that, Thomas left. Katie sat silently a few moments and watched him walk down the hall. Thomas always had an air of not having a thing to do in the world. Never stressed, not in the way she was or other detectives in the unit were. He came from money and had family money waiting for him if he ever left police work. Maybe she'd be that calm and stress free, too, if she had piles of cash to fall back on. But that wasn't how it was. For her, there was nothing else. It was either this or finding some job in customer service, the field she'd been working in before entering the academy.

She stood up and went out to the bull pen. The murder board, a large transparent board on one wall that held all the homicides currently open in the unit, was emptier today. Carter and Richards had both been taken off, this morning. Another pair of detectives, Gibson Duce and Dan Ing, had cleared two other homicides, though not through their own work. Both had been ruled drug overdoses by the ME.

The board was the focus of the unit. As the board shrank, their superiors and administrators grew happier. Gratitude was dispersed, time off was given liberally, and certain perks were distributed. As the board grew full, those things disappeared. The captains and lieutenants grew crankier and less able to help when resources were asked for. The board determined the atmosphere of the unit, something Katie disliked intensely. It put enormous pressure on the detectives to clear homicides that perhaps weren't ready to be cleared, ones where every lead hadn't yet been exhausted. But she felt she was just one cog in a massive wheel and didn't have the power to change the entire culture of the unit, so she kept her head down and did the best she could.

Her captain, Nathan Setter, stuck his head out of his office and said, "Katie, come in here, would you please?"

She went over. His office was far larger than hers, with windows that looked down over the city streets. He had no photos, no decorations other than a coffee mug: "World's Greatest Dad." Nate shut the door behind her and then sat down.

"I was just talking to Thomas about that Richards case and he mentioned you were still working on the Carter matter."

It wasn't lost on her that he had used the word "case" to describe Richards and "matter" to describe Reginald Carter, as though it didn't even warrant being called a homicide case any longer.

"I'm just looking into a few things."

"Like what?"

Katie debated whether to tell him about the photo, but in the end she decided they would find out anyway. "There's a stack of photos we found. They have additional girls in the pictures that weren't at the home. I think Thomas already told you that. But what he didn't tell you, because I haven't shared this with him yet, is that some of the photos had a second set of hands in them. Someone was helping him."

Nate didn't move, as though what she'd just said didn't hold any interest for him. "A set of hands? You sure they're not Carter's hands?"

"Well, someone had to take the photo. We're talking old Polaroids."

He shrugged. "They had timers on the cameras as far back as I remember. Any distinctive marks on the hands?"

"No. Not that you can see from the picture."

"Then I think we assume it's Carter's hands and move on."

"Why would we assume that? Shouldn't we assume it's someone else and look into it?"

Setter folded his hands on the desk and leaned forward. "Katie, this case has brought a lot of pain to a lot of people. When we closed it, we alleviated some of that pain. Do you really want to open those wounds back up just because you have a set of hands in a photo? Haven't those poor people been through enough?"

"Nate, don't bullshit me. There's no closure for families of homicides. It doesn't happen. What is this really about?"

He looked away. "I'm just saying the case is over and done with."

"The case, or the media attention? There'd be a lot of pressure to make sure this case wasn't opened again. I bet the chief caught some flack over a serial killer working for thirty years in his city without us even having a hint about it."

"You think what you want, but bottom line, this case is done."

"What does it hurt if I follow up for a couple of weeks? I won't let it interfere with anything else."

He shook his head. "No, it's done. It's off the board, and the assistant chief himself came down here to congratulate everybody."

"I can't believe it. He was right."

"Who was?"

She swallowed and looked out the window. A handful of cars were stuck at a red light at the intersection. "Fine. It's over."

He nodded and grinned. "It's for the best."

She headed out to her office. Though she was loath to spend what little time off she had working a case, the captain had just given her no choice. Reginald Carter and his partner suddenly became a priority.

28

Stanton's hand went to his firearm, then he pulled it away. If this wasn't the right place, or even if it was and Tad wasn't the man Jack had described, he didn't want a gun involved. He had no intention of terrifying someone who didn't deserve it.

At the top of the stairs, he peered around a corner. He was in the kitchen now. The linoleum was old, dull white and orange and coated in stains. A dining table was built into a nook and a paper plate with some leftover chicken sat next to an empty bottle of beer. Stanton stepped around the corner and leaned against the sink, listening to the noises of the home. He didn't hear anything but the rain against the window behind him.

He crossed the kitchen and slowly stepped into the hallway between the kitchen and the living room. The furniture, like the linoleum, was at least fifty years out of date. Black-and-white photos sat on the mantel, and Stanton looked at each one. Several had an older woman with a young boy. The place seemed to be owned by someone from that generation, and he guessed Tad Lockwood lived with his grandmother.

The television in the living room was ancient and still had the bunny-ears antennae Stanton remembered from his youth. He ran his fingers lightly over the smooth metal, a grin on his face as he remembered hundreds of hours in front of a television like this one, watching cartoons and *Alf* and *Who's the Boss?* His sister's favorite had been *The Facts of Life*, one he could never get into.

Stanton glanced out the front room's window and saw his Jeep at the curb. It seemed out of place in this neighborhood. He suddenly became aware that all the cars were older-model Cadillacs, Lincolns, and Oldsmobiles. Much like the house, the cars were from a different generation, too.

Lying out on the coffee table were some magazines, mostly ones you might find at a police station about guns, hunting, or forensics, and a few pieces of mail. He lifted the envelopes and flipped through them. All of them were addressed to Thaddeus J. Lockwood. He threw them back on the coffee table and headed to the hallway leading to the bedrooms.

The first bedroom on the left was pink. The carpet, bedspreads, and curtains were pink. Women's shoes lined the wall on one side, coated with a thick layer of dust. A dresser on the far end of the room had a few more old photos sitting on top of a white doily. Stanton quickly glanced over them. This batch had more people than in the living room, but the boy and the old woman were still prominent.

The next room down the hallway was the bathroom, and Stanton took only a cursory glance around before looking in the medicine cabinet. A few prescriptions for anti-anxiety medication made out to Tad, and bottles of sleeping pills, but nothing out of the ordinary.

The last room was a much larger bedroom than the other one. A bed took up most of the room. The window looking out on the backyard was covered in thick, heavy curtains, blocking out the light entirely. Inside the closet, Stanton saw an array of men's clothing. He ran his hand over them, getting a feel for each one. The clothes were not meant to impress. They consisted of T-shirts, tank tops, and hoodies without logos—clothing meant only for functionality and comfort.

The room had no photos, no television or radio, no phone or even lamps. A small bathroom off to the side was empty. As Stanton stepped out of the bathroom, he noticed the knob on the door. It wasn't a standard knob with a small lock like the other bedroom. The lock looked industrial, heavy steel, and locked from outside the room. As Stanton bent down and looked at it, he heard something.

It was a small sound, almost like a scratch against a wall or ceiling. He froze, even holding his breath, and his eyes closed as he focused every ounce of mental energy on listening. He waited a long time, five or six minutes, taking only small, shallow breaths so his breathing wouldn't interfere with the sound, but there was nothing else.

Stanton rose and scanned the room again. Someone had put a lock on the outside of this door, hoping to keep someone else in it. His first thought was that maybe Tad's grandmother used to lock him in this room as a child. It was a pattern he'd seen many times before. The sadistic grandparents became the de facto caretakers when something happened to the parents and tortured the helpless child. Sometimes they created monsters.

Stanton had had a friend named David. David was mercilessly picked on at school, beaten to a pulp nearly every day. Stanton felt sorry for him and walked him home one day so he wouldn't be alone. When they got to his house, his grandmother was furious that he had gotten blood on his shirt, and she made him drop his trousers right there in front of Stanton, and beat him with a coat hanger. David didn't cry. Later, he told Stanton that his grandmother wanted him to cry, so he never did. He held it in as much as he could.

One day David, ten years old at the time, waited until his grandmother was in the bathtub. David went into the kitchen, retrieved the largest knife he could comfortably carry, and slowly entered the bathroom while his grandmother bathed.

Stanton was too young to understand the details, and most of it was kept from him, but Elizabeth had told him that she overheard their parents discussing it. David's grandmother had been found with a stab wound to the chest. She survived, and David was taken to juvenile detention.

Stanton wondered if Tad Lockwood was like David, trapped in a house with a monster who was supposed to love him.

He was turning away when he happened to glance down and see the box under the bed.

The box was made of solid wood. Now that he focused his attention on it, he could see that the bed had been raised to allow for more room underneath. Stanton bent down and pulled the box out. It was heavy, too heavy to pull with one hand. He had to squat down and use both hands and his legs and back to pull it out… and then he heard it.

A yelp. Maybe a natural noise the wood made by being pulled out with something so heavy inside, but he didn't think so.

He put his ear against it and listened; inside, he heard the sound he most dreaded to hear at that moment: breathing. Someone was inside the box. On the corners were small grates, probably to let in air, and he put his mouth close to it.

"This is the police. Is someone in there?"

No response at first, and then just a soft whine—a child's whine.

Stanton rose and ran into the kitchen. He looked for anything that could break open the lock on the box, though he hadn't actually seen one. But how else could it stay closed without the child opening it?

He found a set of tools in a cupboard next to the sink and grabbed a hammer and a flathead screwdriver before running back to the bedroom. Searching all the edges of the box, he didn't see a lock. He lifted the box slightly and looked underneath; no lock there either. Slowly, he lifted the lid and it came off.

Inside, a young girl had her eyes closed, tears running down her cheeks. Her clothes were in tatters and blood and urine had stained her legs. It wasn't locked. She was so frightened that she willingly stayed in the box.

"It's okay," he said, "it's okay. I'm a police officer. My name is Jon."

She wouldn't open her eyes. He lightly touched her hand and she recoiled and screamed. He was about to call in an ambulance when he heard boots against the floor behind him, turning just in time to see Tad Lockwood swinging a baseball bat at his head.

Stanton only had time to raise his arm. The bat slammed into his forearm and elbow, sending a rush of burning pain through his arm. The impact knocked him onto his back.

Tad lifted the bat with a scream and slammed it down into Stanton's torso. Stanton felt the impact like a truck and groaned as his body curled up instinctively. Tad raised the bat again and swung down, this time aiming for his skull.

Stanton twisted to his right and the bat hit the floor and his shoulder. He rolled back over, grabbing the bat so Tad couldn't lift it, and kicked into his groin as hard as he could. Tad recoiled and Stanton kicked again, forcing his leg up with everything he had. It was enough to send the man back a few steps.

The bat was still in Stanton's hand. He stood up to swing just as Tad tackled him and they both went down, slamming into a dresser, carving out a hole in the drywall. Stanton came up with a knee into Tad's groin again. Tad yelped and both his hands went down.

Stanton reached down and grabbed the man's genitals. He could feel them through the soft basketball shorts the man had on. He twisted and squeezed as hard as he could, not stopping when Tad screamed and struck him. Tad hit him again and again, but Stanton wouldn't let go. He twisted so far he felt the testicles rupture in his hand. Tad couldn't handle any more. He fought to get away.

Stanton let him go, and the man made a run for the door. Stanton pulled out his firearm and fired a single round. It went straight through Tad's arm. The impact threw him into the wall and he bounced off and hit the floor, lying on top of the girl, who was now screaming hysterically.

Tad bled on the box, screaming and shouting. Stanton took out his cell phone with one hand, the other holding the gun pointed at Tad's head. He felt the smoothness of the trigger, the weight of the gun, and saw the young girl's terrified face. He wanted nothing more than to pull that trigger, but the 911 operator was already on the line.

"I need an ambulance. I've shot someone."

29

The room was cold. Stanton had never realized how cold an interrogation room could be. Most rooms in larger precincts had their own separate temperature controls so they could literally turn up the heat—the detectives would let the suspects cook in high temperatures before interviewing them, building a desire to want to leave at any cost.

But the room's heat hadn't been turned on. In fact, not much of anything had happened in the past two hours. Stanton had been left here staring at the walls. He didn't mind. He needed time to process what had happened. Though his arm ached, the paramedics had confirmed it wasn't broken. Only his nerves appeared to be affected by his encounter with Tad Lockwood.

Stanton closed his eyes, emptying his mind. The mind—the "mad monkey," as Hindu monks called it—would run wild if allowed. To truly focus, it had to be empty. Devoid of memories, emotions, and thoughts. As he sat in the cold interrogation room, it all fell away. The walls and ceiling, the sidewalks and buildings, the city and country, the planet… He was adrift in a sea of stars high above everything else. Relaxed. He could see it so clearly that he felt it.

And then the door opened, and the universe of calm shattered. Stanton opened his eyes but didn't turn around as Thomas Garcia walked in and sat across from him. He sat quietly at first and then leaned back in the seat with a grin.

"You shot an unarmed man," Thomas said.

"I already gave my statement."

"Oh, I know. I read it several times. Makes you out to be a hero, don't it?"

"No, it's the truth."

"The truth," he scoffed. "Truth is a funny thing. Changes depending on who you ask. 'Cause Tad, he's got a different version of the truth. According to him, you broke into his house and assaulted him and his daughter."

"That's not his daughter."

"Adopted daughter, yes it is."

Stanton held his gaze. "Have you seen her?"

"No."

"There's blood caked to her legs. It's from the multiple times he raped and sodomized her. He kept her in box, like a toy he could bring out whenever he wanted. So either you're a complete incompetent and don't realize what you have on your hands, or you're going to lie to me to try to get me to confess to something that isn't true."

Thomas grinned. "We found video of three other girls, too. They're relatively recent."

"Men like him adopt girls and rent them in their communities for short periods."

Thomas leaned forward. "You should've put the bullet in his head, not his arm," he whispered.

Stanton held his gaze. "I tried," he said softly.

Thomas leaned back in his seat, back on the hind legs of the chair like a boy bored at school. "Still, you did shoot an unarmed man."

"No DA would ever prosecute me for that. The media would destroy him. He'd be seen as sticking up for the rights of child rapists."

He nodded. "Yeah, you're right, but for now, I get to keep you here."

The two men sat staring at each other a long while before the door opened behind them. Katie stood for a moment and then approached Thomas, standing over him like a mother scolding a child.

"What the hell do you think you're doing?"

"Katie, I love you, but you don't get to—"

"We found some more photos at the home. Of Tad with Carter. He's the second man."

Thomas stared at her silently.

"Leave him alone," she said. "He just solved a case you didn't think existed. You can go take credit for it now in front of the cameras."

Reluctantly, and with his eyes fixed on Stanton, he rose and left the room. Katie took his place.

"I'm sorry," Stanton said. "I don't like causing tension between partners."

"He sold me out when he went to the captain and told him I was on a wild goose chase. He doesn't trust my judgment. Probably because I'm 'a woman in a man's field.'" She paused. "I'm... sorry I didn't help more. If you hadn't pushed so hard, we never would've caught him. And that poor girl... Anyway. He's being taken into custody by the FBI tomorrow morning. Some of the girls in the videos are missing."

Stanton nodded. "The feds will take this one over. It's for the best. You don't want just Tad, you want the entire ring he's involved in. The

FBI's got better resources for that."

"Maybe, I don't know. I thought it'd be interesting to pursue it. I'm sick of investigating drive-by shootings."

"This isn't a case you want to be involved in, Katie. You could lose yourself in something like this."

"You don't think I can handle it?"

"No, you can handle it. I'm just trying to save you the pain."

She folded her arms. "You see me the same way Thomas does, don't you? Someone you need to protect."

"I didn't mean it that way," Stanton said. "I'm just… really tired. I need to get some sleep."

She sighed. "I'm sorry. I didn't mean it like that either. It's just hard when everyone treats you like you need protecting."

Stanton rose. "Where is Tad now?"

"St. Mark's Hospital. Until the feds take custody. Why?"

"Just curious." He stood there a moment, wanted to say something, but wasn't sure what. So instead he just said, "I appreciate everything you did."

"Sure. Hey, if you're ever in town again, maybe hit me up for a cup of coffee or something?"

He grinned. "Sure. I'll… I'll see ya," was all he could manage to say.

"Yeah, see ya."

Stanton left the interrogation room and went out into the bull pen. The detectives and several uniformed officers stared quietly a second before they clapped. He nodded sheepishly and said, "Thank you," as he tried to make his way through them and to the door. A few people slapped his back, and another detective was pouring drinks out of a thermos. Plastic cups were passed around, and on the monitor of one of the computers, Stanton saw the first page of the *Seattle Times*. It read, "Monster of Hill Park Had Accomplice. Police Make Arrest As FBI Is Called In."

Celebrations were rare in a homicide unit. Most murders were solved because several witnesses saw what occurred and pointed the finger. The ones that took longer than forty-eight hours almost never resulted in an arrest. The sheer volume of unsolved homicides in any major city ground away at the detectives' morale. Stanton wouldn't deprive them of a victory.

He stayed and chatted, going through how he discovered Tad and what went through his mind as he entered the home without backup. Several of the detectives said they were owed favors by the DA and would make sure he was never charged with anything. Stanton thanked them and quietly left the building.

When he was outside, staring up at the gray sky and grateful that he would soon have some sunshine, he heard footsteps behind him and turned to see Katie running out to him.

"Hey," she said.

He grinned. "Hey."

"I know this is stupid, but… do you wanna have dinner with me tonight?"

"I would love to."

She smiled, leaned forward, and pecked him on the cheek. As she returned to the building, he stood and watched her a while. Suddenly, the gray skies didn't seem so bad.

30

Dinner would be at the Dahlia Lounge. Katie said she could meet him at seven, which worked well for Stanton because he had one more thing to do before he could put this behind him: he had to know how Elizabeth had died.

In the parking lot of St. Mark's Hospital, he debated whether to leave, starting his Jeep several times and then turning it off again. The sunlight never broke through, and he wished he was on a beach somewhere, the ocean rolling in. He thought better near the water and with sunlight on his face.

Finally, after nearly half an hour, he got out of the Jeep and strode inside the hospital. He asked the receptionist where Tad Lockwood's room was and showed her his badge.

"That's from Honolulu," she said.

Stanton put the badge away. "I'm consulting on his case."

He said nothing more. Most people talked too much and got themselves into trouble in situations that called for discretion. The woman mumbled something and pressed a button.

"Heather, another detective to see Mr. Lockwood."

"Thank you," he said.

She leaned forward and whispered, "I wish sometimes we had the death penalty up here. If anyone deserves it…"

Stanton didn't say anything but nodded as though he agreed with her.

A nurse came in, heavyset with glasses hanging around her neck on a thin chain. "Come with me, Detective," she said, as though taking Stanton back would exhaust her.

They walked down a corridor and stopped in front of a room with a uniformed officer sitting in front. Stanton thanked the nurse and showed the officer his badge.

"I've been consulting with Detective Wong. I was hoping I could talk to Tad before the feds took him tomorrow."

"Sorry, Detective," the officer said. "Love to help, but I have orders from on high that no one's supposed to see him until the FBI gets here. They want him fresh."

"No, they don't. They don't trust local law enforcement. They think we'll screw up the interrogation and he'll walk." Stanton sat on a chair next to the officer. "One of the girls he killed was my sister. I just have to know… I just have to know how she died. I have to."

The officer stared at him, a look of pure sympathy in his eyes as though Stanton was a man walking to the gallows. "You sure you wanna know?"

He nodded.

"Okay," the officer said, "go on back."

Stanton rose, his knees like Jell-O, his stomach in knots. So many nights had been spent wondering what the man who killed Elizabeth was like; where he was, what he was doing. Stanton knew Carter, and now he would put a second face to the crime. He wondered if those faces would ever leave him. Once he learned how she died, what she went through, how could he possibly think about anything else? Over time, maybe, he would learn to deal with it.

He took a deep breath and stepped inside the room.

31

Congratulating Stanton had turned into an excuse for the detectives to have a shot of whiskey at work. Captain Setter didn't mind as long as the detectives didn't get drunk and didn't have any witnesses to interview that afternoon.

Katie sat with them, listening to their war stories, the descriptions of cases that stuck with them. Almost all of them were humorous, but those weren't the ones that kept her up at night. The ones she remembered most were the ones that she didn't talk about with anyone else but that were always there, on the periphery of consciousness like some predator hiding in the shadows waiting for an opportunity to pop out.

One of her first cases had been a seventeen-year-old boy who had been murdered by two ex-cons. The cons threw a party and got the boy drunk. When he refused their sexual advances, they sodomized him for two hours. They didn't intentionally kill him; with a blood alcohol level in the toxic zone, the boy blacked out and choked on his own vomit. Others at the party had told the detectives that the men were laughing about the rape. They thought it was one of the funniest things they'd ever done.

When Katie finally saw the boy the next day, she was amazed how white a body could get, how blue the lips would become upon death. Within a matter of hours after death, the boy looked like an inanimate object, like a table or tree. Whatever moved the flesh had vanished.

"Katie," the captain said, "in my office, please."

Katie rose and went to Nathan's office. Seated across from him was a man she'd never seen: tall and thin with gray hair and a black suit.

"This is Agent Roosevelt with the FBI. He's going to be picking up Tad and just wanted to confer with the detectives on the case."

Katie offered her hand and Roosevelt took it. "Nice to meet you," she said.

"You, too."

"Well," she said, folding her arms and choosing not to sit, "what do you need to know?"

"We tried interviewing the girl, but she's too far gone right now. She just started screaming and crying."

Katie said nothing, though he seemed to be waiting for a reaction from her. When none came, he continued.

"We were told one of the victim's family members discovered Mr. Lockwood's involvement."

"Yes, he's a detective with Honolulu PD. What about him?"

"Is it true he broke into the home?"

Katie looked from one man to the other. "What does it matter?"

Nathan said, "It matters, because if it's an illegal search, every shred of evidence inside the home is going to be tossed."

Katie's heart dropped. "He's not a government agent in this state. They can't do that."

Roosevelt held up his hand as though interjecting. "Nothing's certain yet. And you'd be hard pressed to find a judge to overturn this in the trial court, but on appeal, there is a possibility. If this man was acting on his own, then the search will be valid. But because he's a cop, and he was consulting with you on the case, an argument could be made that he was under direct supervision by the Seattle PD."

"That's bullshit," she exclaimed. "I didn't know he was going to do that, and if I did, I would've stopped him."

Nathan said, "No one's blaming anyone, Katie. He acted irrationally, and this is on him if this guy walks."

"Irrationally? Have you ever had a member of your family murdered, Captain?"

Nathan and Roosevelt both glanced at each other but didn't say anything. Katie knew this was some unspoken truth between them. They had probably sat in this office attacking Jon Stanton's actions, not willing to acknowledge that he was a man in immense pain who had been pushed to this and that, ultimately, they would probably have done the same thing in his shoes.

"Katie," Nathan finally said, "no one's denying what he's gone through. We just question his judgment. He should've come to you. We would've looked into the guy, found some way to get a warrant, and everything would've been on the up-and-up."

Katie, anger welling inside of her, had to bite her tongue. The only thing she said was, "I think there's a ten-year-old girl who disagrees with you."

She left the office and headed out of the precinct. She needed to be alone. Sometimes things occurred on the job that dug deep inside her like a worm crawling through her veins. Several times every year, she found herself asking why exactly she remained a cop.

"Hey, where you going?" Thomas said, jogging to catch up with her.

"Up yours, Tom."

"Easy. What the hell did I do?"

"You got the feds involved? Who does that behind their partner's back?"

"Whoa, whoa, will you stop a second?" He ran in front of her, blocking her path. "Are you crazy? I would never bring those pricks in."

"You told Nathan about Jon and me looking into this."

"He asked what I was doing. He's our captain. Besides, how was I supposed to know the Lone Ranger was planning on breaking into someone's house? I didn't think anything of it. I would never rat you out. Ever."

She exhaled, her hands on her hips as she paced the corridor. "They're going to arrest him. The charges probably won't stick, or they'll be bargained down to a misdemeanor, but Nathan and the feds want to send a message that they don't condone this type of thing."

He shrugged. "What can we do?"

"Just let me know what the feds have planned. I need to go talk to him. I think he's doing something right now that might dig a deeper hole."

32

Stanton shut the door behind him.

The hospital room looked like any other, except it had no windows.

Tad Lockwood was handcuffed to the hospital bed. The television blared some daytime talk show, and Stanton turned it off. Tad didn't react. He grinned as Stanton pulled up a chair and sat next to the bed.

"My arm fuckin' hurts," Tad said.

"I've got a purple bruise in the shape of a bat up to my shoulder. We're even."

Tad turned his gaze back to the television though it wasn't on. "They find the videos?"

"They did."

He nodded. "That's too bad. You do somethin' long enough, and you don't think you'll ever get caught, ya know? Like you're just too smart for 'em." Tad looked over. "You're not recording this?"

"No. This isn't an interrogation. I just want to talk."

Tad adjusted his head on the pillow, averting his eyes from Stanton's and staring up at the ceiling. "I had the sickness since I was seventeen."

"The sickness?"

"Yeah. That's what I called it. Some folks, they try and bullshit themselves. Tell themselves what we do is normal. Like there ain't nothin' wrong with it. I never bullshit myself. I knew I was sick; I couldn't help it. I was born this way."

Stanton hesitated a moment before asking. "Did you know Reginald Carter?"

Tad nodded.

"You helped him with some of the girls?"

Tad nodded again.

Stanton, his fingers trembling, reached into his jacket and retrieved a photo. It was laminated but still creased at the edges and fading. Stanton stared at it a long time and suddenly became aware that he was neither blinking nor breathing. "This is my sister," he said, handing Tad the photo. "Did you and he… Did you kill her, Tad?"

Tad examined the photo. "No. It weren't me. Reggie was there, but it weren't him neither."

"Please tell me the truth. It stays between us. I just need to know. It's affected me deeper than anything else in my life. I have to know what happened. I know you're sick, but you're still human."

Tad swallowed and handed the photo back. "It weren't me… I wasn't the only one."

Stanton felt himself more acutely in the moment than at almost any other point in his life. The way his clothing rubbed against his skin, the pressure on his legs and buttocks from sitting.

"There's a third person," he whispered.

Tad nodded.

"Who?" Stanton said, on his feet now, towering over the man. "Who is he, Tad? Who killed my sister?"

Tad now held his gaze, the two men staring at each other for a second in silence before Tad said, "You already know. He told me you talked to him and he was worried."

"The only person I've ta—"

Stanton felt sick, as if he'd been spun on a rollercoaster, stepped off quickly, and tried to walk. His stomach tied up in a knot and he felt dizzy. He sat down in the chair, staring at the man before him. Tad looked weak now, almost frail. He had seemed like a monster back at the house, but he wasn't a monster. He was just a human being, a man with drives and hopes and dreams. And that, Stanton thought, was the most frightening part of the darkness. That it could hide in a normal body, and even a normal life, yet still control everything.

Stanton rose to his feet and rushed out of the room without a word.

33

The Jeep couldn't go fast enough. Though he didn't want to get pulled over, Stanton ignored stop signs and red lights when he could. Even then, the drive seemed to take forever.

He couldn't let his thoughts drift too much. All he felt was guilt and shame. How had he not seen this sooner? How had his father not seen it? The weight of it was too much. It seemed the world was closing in around him, so he focused. He focused on the road and the lines to the side of the Jeep as he sped past. He focused on the other cars, on the sky, on the trees, on the signs that turned to little more than blurry flashes of color. When he finally glanced down at his speedometer, he was pushing ninety-five.

Stanton slowed down and tried to calm himself. Once he pulled off the interstate and was back in Rosebud, he sped again, all the way through the neighborhoods until he slammed on his brakes in front of the Browns' home. From here, he could see his own childhood home.

Jumping out of the Jeep, he rushed to the front door, pulling out his Desert Eagle and holding it low. He pressed his ear against the door and listened for a while before leaning back and slamming his foot near the doorknob. The door was too thick; it barely moved. He ran around to the side door and smashed through it with his shoulder, the edge of the door splintering and raining slivers over the carpet. He held his weapon up, perfectly in alignment with his shoulder, his head up and in line with his spine. It was instinctive for him after fifteen years; he didn't have to think about his stance or his breathing or when he would or wouldn't pull the trigger. In a way, it felt as though it was out of his hands.

He stepped into the kitchen, slipping off his shoes to make less noise. The house was quiet. Every few seconds he paused and listened, but he didn't hear anything. He came around to the stairs leading to the second level and then wondered if anyone was even there.

"Dale?" he shouted. "You home?" He tried to sound as innocuous as possible, as though just dropping by for a visit. "Dale, I was hoping we could get something to eat. I wanted to ask you something about my dad." He opened the door of a closet, peered inside, and then pointed his firearm inside. The closet held several coats, some of them women's and children's coats. He scanned them and then split them apart to look behind them.

"Dale," he yelled again, "please come out. I'm leaving for Honolulu and just wanted to chat again before I go."

Stanton took the stairs leading up to the second floor. They led to a long hallway and bedrooms on either side. The first was a child's room, untouched in decades. Even the sheets were still on the bed, posters up on the wall. Another next to it the same as the first, and then a master bedroom with a large bed and a balcony. He poked his head into the bedroom and peered around a dresser before stepping inside. On the east side of the room was a walk-in closet, and Stanton went over to it. He held his breath, leaned against the wall, and opened the closet door before peeking inside quickly. Empty on first glance. As he was about to go in and explore further, he saw something on the dresser: a sheet of paper with scribbling on it.

Stanton picked up the sheet of paper. All it said was, "Jon, I'm sorry. Goodbye."

Underneath the dresser, he noticed something by his foot. He picked up a strip of duct tape. Stanton got down flat on his stomach and looked under the bed to find a box just like the one at Tad Lockwood's house. He pulled it out and ripped off the lid. It was empty. The duct tape was from the girl, and Dale had taken her with him.

As Stanton rose, his cell phone rang with an unidentified number. He answered.

"This is Jon."

A long silence, and then, "I'm sorry, bud. I really am."

Stanton's heart dropped as he ran to the balcony and wondered if Dale was nearby, watching him. "Where are you, Dale? I'd like to talk."

"I'm sure you would, but I'm not stupid. You can't do what I've done for so long and be stupid."

"What've you done, Dale?"

"I've done some bad things, bud. Some really bad things. I couldn't help it. It was so damn overpowering sometimes. I couldn't eat or sleep unless I did it. I hope you understand."

"Where are you?"

"I can't tell you, and don't ask me again."

Stanton went back inside and rushed downstairs and out the door, hoping to see Dale in a nearby car. "Don't hurt the girl."

"I… I don't know if I can help it. She's my insurance policy for now, though. But only for one day. All right? One day you can't go to

168

the cops or do anything. And I won't kill her for that day."

"And after that day?"

"Well, I don't know. I haven't decided. But if you don't agree, I'll kill her right now." He exhaled into the phone. "Sometimes it don't feel like I'm in charge. I just can't control it. I can't hold it back."

"Dale, listen to me. You can get through this. You don't have to let it in."

"Shoot, you don't have any idea what it's like."

"Yes, I do."

A silence between them.

"Well anyway," Dale said, "you gimme one day, and I don't do nothin' to her for that day. And I'll think about letting her go."

"I'll give you as long as you need." He paused. "Dale, you want me, not her. Let her go and come get me. I won't be armed. I'll just be at your house, alone."

He chuckled. "Want you? Want you for what? I like you, Jonny. I always have. And your daddy, even though he was a miserable son of a bitch sometimes. I don't want to hurt you. But I'm not rotting in a cell getting raped every day, neither. I'll kill her and myself before I do that."

"Just give me a call in a day and let me know she's safe."

"All right. One day."

Stanton hung up. He stood in the road and stared at the wet cement, the way the rain soaked the grass, but didn't glisten as it did in Hawaii. *One day.* He knew what the day was for: just long enough for Dale to escape the state. Though getting better, interstate communication between law enforcement was still shoddy at best. He could be pulled over in Idaho or Nebraska and the "be on the lookout" or BOLO call in Washington might not even show. Stanton couldn't let that happen. He couldn't let him get away with another girl. Not another one.

He jumped into his Jeep and casually pulled away, as though unsure where to go, just in case Dale was watching him from somewhere. But as soon as he hit the interstate, he gunned it straight back to Seattle.

34

Stanton ran into the precinct while he turned on his phone. He'd had it off for the past hour and now saw that Katie had called twice and texted once, wondering where he was. He hoped she was here, but even if she wasn't, Stanton would talk to Thomas. Clearly he didn't like Stanton, but he wouldn't ignore this just because of that dislike.

Stanton hurried past the officer at the front desk and pretended he belonged there. He got all the way to the detective's floor before anyone even asked him if he needed help.

"I know where I'm going, thanks."

He walked into the bull pen and saw Thomas sitting on a desk, chatting with one of the detectives. Stanton walked over. When Thomas saw him, he rolled his eyes.

"What're you doing here?"

"I need to see Katie."

"She went out looking for you."

"Then I need to talk to you. It's urgent."

Thomas sighed and hopped off the desk. "Let's talk in the conference room."

Stanton followed him through the bull pen to a conference room with a large table and high-backed chairs. Thomas sat down, and Stanton sat right next to him. Proximity sometimes bred feelings of likability.

"There was a third man that was helping Carter. I've found him. He was a neighbor of mine growing up, Dale Brown. He's taken off with a girl, probably an adopted girl. By tomorrow, he'll be out of the state and he may kill her because it's easier than traveling with her."

Thomas stared at him a second. "Wait here."

He rose and left the conference room. A minute later, another man walked in and sat down across from Stanton.

"Detective Stanton, my name is Nathan Setter. I'm the captain of the Homicide Unit here. Detective Garcia has explained to me that you believe there was a third man associating with Reginald Carter, is that right?"

Stanton nodded. "Yes, his name is Dale Brown, and his address is—"

Nathan held up his hand, cutting Stanton off. "We can get to all that later. What I really want to know right now is, did you go into his home?"

Stanton looked back and forth between the two men. "Yes."

"Without his permission?"

"He fled with the young girl he was holding prisoner there. That's what we need to focus on."

"The young girl that you think is his daughter."

"Probably. Look, why are you sitting here interviewing me? Let's put out a BOLO on him and any vehicles he drives, call the airports and bus stations—"

"Detective, you broke into a man's house and shot him. An unarmed man. And now you're telling me you broke into another man's house?"

"He was only unarmed after I took away the baseball bat he was trying to break my skull with." Stanton paused. They weren't going to listen to him unless he took a different approach. "Guys, I know this is your turf and you're upset I'm stomping around. I get that. But do what you want with me after we make sure this girl is safe. Please, put out a BOLO call on Dale Brown. If he leaves the state, I'm not sure we'll find him again."

Nathan glanced at Thomas, who shrugged.

"Detective," Nathan said, "I'm afraid it won't be that easy. I'm going to need you to stand up please."

"For what?"

Thomas rose and pulled out the handcuffs clipped to his belt. Stanton laughed. No other reaction seemed appropriate—disbelief, maybe even shock. Few things shocked him anymore. He was surprised that he didn't actually have anything to say. So he just held out his wrists.

"Actually," Nathan said, "that won't be necessary, Tom. Just put him in a holding cell for now. No other inmates."

Thomas put the cuffs away, and Stanton thought he picked up a sense of disappointment from him. But he did take his arm and lead him through the precinct, making sure all the other detectives saw him being led away. They went downstairs to what Stanton knew was the drunk tank, where they kept intoxicated suspects until they sobered up. Stanton could always smell a drunk tank.

"Hope you like our accommodations," Thomas said.

"It's easy to hate, isn't it? It's much harder to be compassionate."

"I don't hate you," he said, leading him into the cell and slamming the door. "I just don't like you."

"I think you'll find, Detective Garcia, that the difference between those two sentiments is slim. And when something becomes the object of your hatred, you'll lose yourself in pursuit of its destruction."

Thomas leaned against the bars, staring at him with a smirk. "See, that's why I don't like you. You don't talk *with* people, you talk *at* them. Like you just know so much more than them."

Stanton stepped close to the bars, never breaking eye contact with him. "I've hated a man for every second of my life since the time I was ten years old. It ate up everything else in my reach, destroyed relationships, careers, haunts me at night… I do know more about hatred than you do."

"I wouldn't worry about acting on it. You're not going anywhere for a while." Thomas held his gaze a bit longer and then left, leaving him staring through bars at an empty hallway.

35

Stanton lay down on the bench and stared at the ceiling. All jails looked the same: plain and depressing. He could hear the patter of rain against the roof and listened to it for a long time, trying to anticipate the rhythm. The lights were fluorescent, which always caused a headache. When one started pounding away in the depths of his skull, he finally closed his eyes.

Several things ran through his mind, and one of the most prominent was what they would charge him with. At best, obstruction of justice and burglary for breaking into the homes. At worst, they could charge him with the attempted murder of Tad Lockwood. It wouldn't stick, it'd be pled down, but it'd be enough to keep him inside a cell and take away his badge forever.

Next to him, he heard a sound. He looked down to see a fly on the steel bench next to him. The fly had been partially smashed and buzzed only sporadically, and he wondered if the fly had been there when he lay down and he'd smashed it, or if it was already like that. Stanton stared at the fly as its buzzing dimmed, and eventually it stopped moving. It seemed fitting somehow that the fly would die here, surrounded by steel and concrete like a giant coffin.

Everything he'd been through and everything he'd done had brought him here. Maybe it was inevitable. His career had ruined two relationships with women he loved deeply. It had alienated him from his sons and, he knew because of the stress and the research done on police officer mortality rates, would take his life too early. And it all stemmed from one man's action thirty years ago.

He pulled out the photo from his jacket. He still had his firearm, too, which was amazing, considering the Seattle PD would be held liable if he happened to fire it while inside. As he'd told Thomas, his hatred would blind him, make him lose focus, and overlook things he should've caught.

Stanton gazed at the photo for a long time. He thought about his first day of school. It wasn't his parents at the doors seeing him off, holding his hand and comforting him. It was Elizabeth. It was always Elizabeth. She was the one who saw his sensitivity and knew he needed extra attention. His father dismissed his sensitivity as weakness, but Elizabeth saw it as strength, as something he could use to help other people. The only way Stanton could describe it was that she saw his soul bare, without any of the defense or pretenses he put up for other people. She knew who he really was in a way no one else ever had. That was the part that he couldn't live with, the part that drove him to blindness, much like Thomas. That part led him to run into the darkness when other detectives were running away from it: the simple belief that the best part of his life had been taken from him, and he could never get it back.

Footsteps echoed in the corridor. Katie turned a corner and strode up to the bars, a guard behind her. He opened the cell and she stepped inside. The guard lingered a moment and she gave him a look, letting him know he wasn't welcome.

"I'll be back at the booth." He shuffled off.

When he was gone, Katie put her hand on his and said, "I'm sorry they did this."

Stanton put his arm over his eyes to shield them from the harsh lights. "I'm not sure they're wrong."

"What do you mean?"

"I can see it so clearly, Katie. It's always been there, and I've never looked at it. Our lives are like an album of pictures, and you just need to look back to see the pattern. I've never done that until now. I see the pattern. I see how blind I've been, how obsessed. And it's destroyed everything around me." He paused. "I don't think I can do it anymore. I'm done. When I get out of here, if I get out of here, I'm going home."

"Now? Thomas told me you think there was a third person."

"There was. But I don't know why it should matter to me. My entire life, I've been chasing ghosts that I'm never going to catch. It doesn't matter."

"So you think this guy's going to kill that girl and you're just not going to do anything?"

"I'm stuck in a cell."

"So? You don't seem like the kind of guy who gives a shit about things like that." She stood up. "It's your choice, Jon. The DA isn't going to file charges against you right now. Carter's case is too fresh in everybody's mind, and the public would be too pissed off if they charged a police officer who saved a little girl. They called Nathan and the chief, and they're letting you go for now. So if you want to go home, you can go home. But if you want to know what happened to Elizabeth, you're going to have to follow him."

Katie turned and walked out of the cell. Stanton watched her go. Everything she had said was true. If he could live without knowing what happened to Elizabeth, he could be on the beach in six hours, letting the waves lap at his ankles, the sunshine browning and invigorating him.

Or he could go into the dark and follow in her footsteps.

Stanton reached into his pocket and pulled out the photo. He had more photos of her—dozens, since he'd inherited them after his mother's death. But this was the only one he remembered being taken. He had stood with her at a mall. They had meant for both of them to be in the picture, but the photographer, a fourteen-year-old friend of Elizabeth's, had screwed up the zoom and it'd only snapped a photo of her. Out of frame, she held his hand as he smiled widely for the camera. Invisible to everyone but her.

He ran the tip of his finger over the photograph, as though he could feel the softness of her cheek. A scent always lingered when she was around, some fruity shampoo or body wash a child of that age would choose. He had never smelled it again and wished desperately to inhale the fragrance one more time. When his mother had passed, he had gone to the house hoping to find that fragrance and instead found his father.

George Stanton looked weak. His skin had paled and the once-mighty forearms that Stanton marveled at as a child were thin and hairless. "There's some things you're going to want," his father had said. "I packed them up for you. They're in your old room."

Stanton retrieved the boxes of photos, albums, and old memorabilia his mother had hung on to. He came down to the living room and saw his father reading a book, flipping so quickly through the pages that Stanton knew he wasn't actually taking in the words.

"I guess I'll be going," he said after loading the boxes in his car.

"Guess so."

"Take care of yourself, Dad."

"You, too."

Stanton stood behind his father, trying to come up with something to say. Something that would establish that connection he'd always yearned for. He hoped it'd be like an electrical wire that was unplugged. Once the connection was reestablished, the current would flow immediately, as though it had never left. But he couldn't think of anything. Nothing seemed appropriate.

"Bye, Dad."

"Bye."

It was the last time Stanton had seen his father alive. He regretted so much in his life, but that moment was one of the most powerful. It woke him at night sometimes. He should've thrown his arms around his father, broken down his layers of defenses and let him know that he had a son. But both of them were too wounded by life's events. And the most painful of those events was Elizabeth's disappearance. And now, Stanton had a chance to put that to rest.

He closed his eyes, said a prayer asking for strength, and then opened his eyes.

Stanton sat up. The motion shifted the blood in his head and made him momentarily dizzy. He let it affect him, let it soak into his mind and enjoyed the sensation for a moment before he got to his feet.

"Katie," he said loudly, "wait."

36

Stanton didn't feel comfortable in the precinct, so they left in Katie's car. She said she needed a coffee, and he sat quietly in the passenger seat and thought as they drove.

"So? What d'you wanna do?" she asked.

"Haven't decided yet."

"We're kind of in a time crunch, aren't we?"

"You ever heard of the Kent Study?"

She shook her head.

"It was a study done at the University of Glasgow to find the most efficient ratio between thought and action to accomplish various tasks. They gave everyone one minute to put together a puzzle or figure their way out of a chess maneuver or other things like that. Then they'd test different ratios on people who had similar IQs. They'd let some people think ten seconds and act for fifty, some were half and half… they tried a lot of different ratios. Do you know what the most efficient was? The one that led to the best outcomes? When they let the participants think for fifty seconds, and act for ten. Almost pure thought. I try to think it through before I act." He paused. "At least, I used to. Before all this came to the surface again."

She put her hand in his and didn't say anything as she drove to a coffee shop down the street.

The coffee shop was packed. Stanton sat at a table by the window and glared at the people coming and going. It was odd that they would be having coffee in the evening, he thought. But caffeine didn't affect everyone the same way.

"You sure you don't want anything?" she asked as she sat back down.

"I'm fine, thanks."

"So have you come up with something?"

"Can you put out a BOLO just in case? All the airports and bus stations, too?"

"Sure. Why 'just in case'? You said he was fleeing the state."

Stanton shook his head, keeping his eyes glued to the window. "I don't know. This is a man who lied to everybody his entire life. He wouldn't tell me the truth, even in a roundabout way. I think he wants me spinning my wheels trying to work with other law enforcement agencies while he hides out somewhere."

"Where?"

"I don't know." He paused, tapping his finger against the table lightly. "He has a son I used to be friends with, Niles. Mind running a search on him?"

She shrugged, taking a sip of coffee. "Sure, why not? Anything else?"

"I need to visit someone else."

When Katie pulled to a stop in front of the house, Stanton didn't get out right away. He looked over at her and gave her what he knew was a sad little smile, just letting her know he appreciated this. Then he stepped out of the car and took the steps to the front door. He was glad Katie didn't follow.

Stanton pulled open a screen door and knocked. A baby was crying inside, and then he heard footsteps and a pause, probably looking out the peephole, and several locks slid open. A portly woman with a baby on her hip looked out over a chain at him.

"Yes?"

"Are you Claire?"

"Yes."

"You don't remember me?"

She stood there a second.

"Jon Stanton. I was… I am Elizabeth's brother."

Her eyes widened, and by the quick movements of her chest Stanton could tell she was breathing harder.

"Jonny?"

The shock dimmed, and as it did so, another little girl, perhaps eight, came around the corner behind her and said, "Mom, who's that?"

"Go to your room, Beth."

"But who is that?"

"I said go to your room."

The girl grunted and turned back around, disappearing from view. When Claire looked at Stanton again, he said, "You named her Beth."

She smiled shyly, then shut the door. Stanton heard a chain slide off, and the door opened wide.

"Come inside," she said.

Though the home was messy, Stanton could tell a lot of care went into it. Photos were aligned perfectly, and several spaces had been set aside for toys. A large color photo of four children took up the wall in the living room, and Claire sat underneath it on an old couch.

"I never thought I would see you again."

Stanton sat down in a recliner. "I didn't come back very often. How have you been?"

"Good. I married David Glenner. You remember him?"

He nodded. "I do. He and his buddies threw me in a garbage can once when he ran into us at a movie theater."

She laughed. "Yeah, that's him. He always liked you, though."

"He's fine. It's funny now." He paused. "I'm sorry to just pop in like this. I never talked to you about what happened."

She swallowed, rocking the baby in her arms gently. "I was interviewed by the police a couple times. I thought there'd be more than that, but there wasn't."

"I read the interviews."

Stanton remembered the anger he had felt the second time he read them. The first time, he hadn't been a detective and didn't know what police reports were supposed to look like. When he went back almost ten years later and read his sister's file, he found that the Missing Persons detectives assigned to her case hadn't even interviewed all the witnesses, and the ones they did interview were asked the most basic questions and hurried through as though the detectives had something more important to do.

"You've heard about Carter?" Stanton said.

She nodded sadly, averting her eyes. "One time, in gym, he tried to come into the locker room when I was changing. He said sorry and pretended like he left, but I could see him peeking around the corner watching me. I never told anyone. Maybe if I had told someone, they woulda done something. Maybe I coulda saved some lives."

"You were a kid," Stanton said. "You didn't know what you were doing."

"I still feel bad."

Stanton's eyes went down to the baby. He couldn't tell if it was a girl or a boy; it was so chubby the rolls covered up its face, and only its eyes poked through the puffy white flesh.

"She wasn't one of his victims. Dale Brown killed my sister."

Her brow furrowed. "Dale Brown? Niles's dad?"

He nodded. "He's gotten away and the police are searching for him. He's the one who picked her up from the movie theater that night."

She hesitated. "That makes sense. We were all just waiting for my mom to pick us up, and this car pulled up and she ran over there. She ran back and told us she had another ride home." She swallowed. "That was the last time I seen her."

"Did my sister say anything else? Anything that Dale had told her?"

Claire shook her head. "No, nothing like that. She just ran back and told us she was leaving."

Something hit Stanton right then that made his heart beat faster, something he couldn't believe he'd never thought of before. "What door did she get into?"

"Door?"

"Yeah. Did she get into the passenger seat or the backseat?"

"Oh. Um, I guess it was the backseat."

If she got into the backseat, then that meant someone was in the passenger seat. Someone that would've made Elizabeth feel more comfortable. It had never sat well with him that his sister just hopped into someone else's car. Even someone she knew. She was smart, the smartest person Stanton had known. There was no way she would willingly do that, unless…

"I gotta go," he said, standing up.

She rose. "I'm so sorry, Jonny. I wish…"

"I know. Thanks for your time."

They hugged, and Stanton sprinted down the steps and out to the car. He jumped inside and said, "Did you get an address for Niles?"

"Yeah."

"Get there as fast as you can," he said, putting on his seat belt.

37

Niles Brown lived in a condo tower overlooking downtown Seattle. Katie sped there, but not as fast as Stanton would've liked. He kept checking the clock on his phone: in sixteen hours, the girl could be dead. The nagging feeling that wouldn't let Stanton go was that she might've already been dead, or Dale might not have plans to kill her at all. But he couldn't risk guessing. He had to move on the assumption that he would kill her and dump her somewhere they would never find her. Maybe the same place Elizabeth was.

Stanton hurried out of the car, not waiting to see if Katie was coming, too. She got out and followed him this time. They waited in the lobby as a security guard checked them in. He called up to the condo and said, "Mr. Brown? The police are here to see you."

Stanton took in the clean, upscale lobby with nearly untouched furniture, the type of place a wealthy bachelor or elderly widower would live. On a table in between two leather couches was an architecture magazine he'd never seen before, with a building on the front cover and a man hanging out his apartment window at least five or six stories up.

"He'll see you now," the guard said.

They took the elevator up nine floors and stepped off. The carpets were beige and clean, and Stanton kept his head down, thoughts whirling in his head until they reached unit 906, Niles's condo.

"I need to talk to him alone," he said.

She looked to the door and then back to him. "Fine. But I hear anything crazy, I'm coming in."

"Just give me five minutes."

Stanton knocked. The door opened and Niles Brown stood there.

He had aged. He was only five years older than Stanton, but Niles looked at least fifteen years older. He had a large belly that hung over his belt, and his hairline receded to nearly past his ears, though he wore his hair forward and down to make up some of the slack. At first he looked annoyed, and then recognition hit him and his mouth nearly fell open. He forced a smile.

"Jon?"

"How are you, Niles?"

"Um, good, man. Good. Come in."

Stanton stepped inside, taking a quick glance at Katie before shutting the door. The condo was elegantly decorated, and soft music played from speakers Stanton couldn't see. Niles lightly touched a black remote on a glass dining table, and the volume decreased. As Stanton crossed over to the living room, he saw a woman wrapped in a sheet and nothing else poke her head out of the bedroom.

"Hope I'm not interrupting," he said.

Niles said. "Not at all. We were done." He went out to the balcony and sat on a chair, and Stanton followed. From the balcony, he could see the entire city sparkling before them as the sun began to set and the man-made lights came on, the sunlight reflecting off the smooth surfaces at sharp angles.

"I thought you'd come back here when I heard about Reggie."

"Yeah, it was a surprise to everyone, I think."

"No shit. My mom just about had a heart attack."

Stanton paused a moment. "Your mother's still alive?"

"Yeah, man. She lives in Tacoma. Why?"

Stanton leaned forward. "Do you remember the night my sister disappeared, Niles?"

Niles pulled out a package of Swisher Sweets and lit one, looking out over the city. "Yeah, man. I remember. I couldn't think about anything else that entire summer. Really fucked me up for a while. I had a huge crush on your sister. We went out once." He smiled. "I kissed her at the Space Needle. I wanted to do more but she wouldn't let me. She wasn't like that."

Stanton put his hands on his thighs, his right hand closer to his firearm in case he needed it, though given the state Niles was in, he didn't think he would. Niles was jittery, sickly, and his eyes were rimmed red. Stanton could smell the strong odor of freshly burnt marijuana, and out on the kitchen counter, he had noticed a bottle of prescription pills.

"One thing that had always bugged me about her disappearance that no one had a good answer for was why she would get into that car willingly. My sister was smart, smarter than me, smarter than my mom or dad. The detectives told us that the driver probably offered her something, or that maybe she knew him. That wasn't enough for me. Even if she knew him, she wouldn't have gotten into that car alone." He paused. "Someone else was in the car with him. Someone who would've made my sister feel safe."

The two men glared at each other a long time. Niles was finally the one who looked away. He set the Swisher down on a small glass table and leaned back in his chair, looking out over the city. "I've tried to kill myself twice, Jon. I can't eat, I can't sleep. I can't have a decent relationship. I'm rich and I've never been so miserable. When you do something that eats you up, you think it gets better over time, but it actually gets worse."

Stanton, his heart in his throat, managed to gasp, "What did you do?"

He fidgeted with his hands, twirling his fingers, rubbing them, pulling on them. Stanton noticed the pads of his fingertips worn away. Several powerful antidepressants had been shown to cause ticks so severe the patient would rub away parts of their flesh, sometimes all the way down to the bone.

"I, ah… My dad… You guys all thought he was so great. You'd come over, you and Shiney, remember him? We called him that because he was bald. He would—"

"Niles," Stanton said, moving closer to him, "what did you do?"

"My dad was a… monster. Remember when I broke my arm right before basketball camp? We were both supposed to go and you said you wouldn't without me and Nate. I told you I fell off my bike, but that's not what happened. At the dinner table, I took a bite of food before my mom was done saying grace. So my dad got his hammer. He held my arm down on the table, right there in front of everyone, and smashed it. Then he sat down and ate." He snorted. "He ate like nothing in the world was wrong, man. What kind of man could do that to his son and then just sit down and eat and talk about work?"

Stanton didn't blink or move. He wasn't entirely sure he could if he wanted to. "I don't know."

"Yeah, man. Yeah… So I moved out when I was eighteen, made a bundle in real estate, became a big shot… and here I am. Still the little boy with the broken arm." He swallowed, his gaze turning to the city before them. "I was there, man. I always wanted to tell you, but my dad said he could hurt my mom and my sister. When I got older, he knew he couldn't threaten me as much anymore, so he'd threaten them. He said if I told anyone about it, he would kill them."

"Tell anyone about what?"

Niles picked up the cigar and took a long puff. The scent was sweet, but had a bitter edge. It had been laced with something. "He picked up Elizabeth from the movie theater that night. I was with him. He made me tell her that we'd just watched a movie and were going for ice cream. When she ran back to her friends, I hoped she told them who she was going with. But she didn't. I don't know what my dad would've done if she had done that. Maybe just had me lie for him, I guess."

"What happened to her, Niles?"

"We have a cabin on Puget Sound. It overlooks the water. Real pretty." He seemed to be elsewhere for a moment. "He never told me what happened. We got to my house and he told me to get out. He grabbed Elizabeth and said he needed to talk to her in private. Then he drove off." Niles looked into his eyes. "It killed me not to tell you. That's why we stopped being friends. That's why I didn't come to her funeral or anything. I couldn't look at you. It'd make me sick and I'd run to the bathroom and throw up."

Stanton's hand slowly slid back to his weapon. He felt the pattern on the metal, the ridges and dips. He opened his fingers wide and pulled his hand away. He stood up. "You're going to tell me exactly where this cabin is."

Niles nodded. "I hope you fucking kill him."

38

Stanton sat in his hotel room alone. He had told Katie bits and pieces, but not the whole picture. He didn't really care if Dale Brown was caught. This was something else, something that had linked the two men forever. Something twenty-seven years in the making.

He cleaned his Desert Eagle then holstered it before getting his jacket. As he checked the fridge for a bottle of water, someone knocked on the door. He waited to see if they would knock again, and they did. Stanton answered the door. Katie stood there, Thomas behind her.

"What's he doing here?" Stanton said.

"He's come to help."

Stanton looked at him. "Help with what?"

Katie folded her arms, as though letting him know he wouldn't be getting past her. "You know where he is, don't you? I could see it on your face when you came out of Niles's condo."

Stanton didn't say anything.

"That's what I thought," she said. "We're going to help."

"You can't."

"Oh, what, is this some macho bullshit about it being between the two of you? You out for revenge, Jon?"

"I don't know."

"Well what's your plan? Just go running up to him and hope he doesn't see it coming? That's crazy."

Stanton relented and took a few steps back, settling into a chair by the door. He stared at the carpet, the way it looked brown in the dim light. "He has a cabin. It's where he took my sister. I bet it's where he has this girl."

Katie came over and bent down, looking him in the eyes. "You don't have to be alone."

"I don't want SWAT or anybody else."

"Why not?"

Thomas said, "Because he wants to kill him."

Stanton looked at him, and then back down at the carpet. He hadn't put the thought into words. It had been more like an urge, like some push inside him that put things in motion to get an outcome. But what that outcome exactly was, Stanton hadn't thought about concretely until just now.

"Seriously?" Katie said. "You would risk everything just for revenge?"

He shook his head. "I don't... I don't know. I just have to go there."

She stood up. "Well, we're coming with you."

The address Niles had given him led up a winding road. The darkness in this section of Washington was nearly complete, with no street lamps, no moon, and no lights on in the homes they passed. The headlights illuminated about twenty feet, and past that was nothing but black: a forest with a few homes thrown in.

Stanton had never been here. He'd never even known this section of the city existed. It covered a massive hill, and the homes looked to be enormously expensive. Considering how modest the Browns' home was, he guessed that Dale Brown had spent more on this cabin than he had on his family's home.

Thomas was driving a black BMW, and the inside was cleaner than almost any car Stanton had ever ridden in. Freshly washed, maybe even washed and vacuumed every day. Katie sat up front with him, and the two leaned toward each other rather than away from each other. Stanton guessed there was either a relationship there that had fizzled out or one that went unrecognized.

Thomas pulled the car over to the side of the road. They were at the peak of the hill, at least a hundred feet away from any other homes. The cabin had a manicured garden out front, the lawn freshly mowed though it must've been done in the rain. Dale would want to keep this home looking like every other. Nothing out of place, not even the grass.

"I'll get the back," Thomas said. "Katie, you run the east side." He looked back at Stanton. "I figured you'd want to go in front."

"I do."

"For the record, this is a mistake. We should have SWAT here."

Stanton shook his head. "No."

They had no reason to listen to him. Thomas or Katie could've easily called in SWAT, and there was nothing Stanton could've done about it. But for some reason they didn't. He figured they saw something here, too, some unfinished business that they knew he had to resolve. No doubt they would change their minds when he entered the house and call it in, but by then it wouldn't matter. Either he would be dead, or Dale would.

Stanton stepped out of the car. The air was cold. Not cool as it had been, but cold like a winter chill. They were near the water and high up, no structures blocking the wind. Stanton hurried to the cabin without waiting for them. The front door was locked, as was the window that probably led to the front room. Out of the corner of his eye, he saw Thomas run silently around the house. Katie went the other way and was just as quiet, her firearm held low.

Even here, on the outskirts of civilization, Dale wouldn't have the girl in the front room. She would be in either the basement or the attic. Stanton scanned the building as he snuck around but didn't see any basement windows. He went around back and saw Thomas standing in front of the back door.

"Locked," he whispered. "Heavy fucker, too. Probably reinforced."

"I don't think we're going in with surprise."

Thomas shook his head. "SWAT could be here in twenty minutes. Let them handle it."

"This isn't about that anymore." Stanton backed up a few paces, holstered his firearm, and sprinted at the house. He felt his legs pumping on the grass and it felt good. The wind whipped his face and was loud in his ears. A large window next to the door probably led into the bedroom. Curtains ran across it, and he couldn't see what was on the other side. He didn't care.

He leapt and covered his face with his arms.

39

It had grown cold. Niles Brown sat on the balcony so long he was shivering. But it didn't bother him. Not much of anything bothered him anymore. Today alone he had ingested Quaaludes and Xanax, smoked several blunts, and drunk enough alcohol to black out once around noon. It mellowed him out so much he would've lain on the couch and drooled had he not taken in a mound of cocaine to counteract the lethargic effects of the 'ludes and pot.

He woke up with one of his favorite prostitutes, Jennifer, though he didn't remember calling her. She said he had and was crying on the phone, though he suspected she was just saying that. Sometimes they just popped in, charged their two grand, and left, leaving him wondering how long they thought they could milk him for.

The door opened behind him, but he didn't turn around. There were only two people that had a key to his condo: Jennifer, who was still in the shower, and... *him*. The shadow of his life. Throughout everything, every pain and joy, every success and failure, every thought of suicide and every thought of elation, the shadow was there. Just on the periphery. Influencing events, influencing him. He could never seem to counter it. It was like quicksand; the more he fought, the more entangled Niles became with it.

Dale Brown sat down next to him, right where Jon Stanton had been sitting not an hour ago, and put his boots up on the railing. He exhaled as though he'd been working hard all day and just needed a break before heading back to the grind. But really, Niles knew, he didn't work. He didn't do anything… except one thing.

"Jon was here," Dale said, his eyes on the twinkling lights of the city.

"Yeah."

"What'd he want?"

Niles tried to seem as casual as possible, as though this were the most normal conversation a father and son could have. But in his mind, he was screaming. He couldn't handle this. Jon Stanton had always been nice to him. Nate, Niles's younger brother, had been frail in school, picked on because he had a good mind and didn't care about the trivial things others their age cared about, like sports and girls.

One of the football players in junior high school, a gorilla named Rick, slammed Nate into the ground one day and stuck his knee into his back. He lifted his head and slammed his face into the ground while shouting, "Lick it! Lick it!" Nate had no choice. In front of everyone there, he licked the ground. He told Niles years later he remembered the taste: salty with beads of dirt that rolled off the linoleum onto his tongue. It was then that Jon sprinted through the hall and jumped at Rick. Stanton was small, not much meat on him, but he threw everything he had at Rick and hit Rick's face, snapping his head back and causing him to topple over. Stanton got on top of him and went to hit him, but when he saw that Rick was crying, probably from a broken nose, he climbed off and left him alone.

No one had expected Stanton to do that. Like Nate and Niles, he didn't play any sports, or at least wasn't any good at them, didn't socialize much, and kept to himself at lunch and recess. But he'd always stuck up for Nate, and Niles had never forgotten it.

"Leave him alone," Niles said.

Dale turned to him. "What did you say?"

Niles, his hands trembling, managed to get out, "I said leave him alone."

Dale was quiet a moment and then burst out laughing. "You ungrateful little shit." Dale leaned forward, grabbing Niles's hand. "What did you tell him?"

Niles recoiled at the touch. As a child, Dale would take his hand and squeeze as hard as he could, sending him to the hospital twice with fractures. As an adult, it wasn't any different. "Don't," Niles said halfheartedly.

"Don't what?" Dale said, squeezing.

"Please don't."

"Don't what?"

The pressure grew intense. Fire shot up from his hand, but Niles didn't show any reaction other than telling his father to stop. He knew what he wanted: he wanted to see Niles cry. But he wouldn't give him that. Not now. Not again.

"Let me go," Niles said.

"Or what? Hm? What you gonna do, Niles? You going to cry to that whore of a mother of yours?"

"She's not a whore!"

"She is what I say she is."

The pain had intensified to a laser beam focused on either side of his hand. Niles fell to the floor of the balcony. He gripped the railing with his free hand, grimacing, his teeth clenched as his father didn't relent.

"Please," Niles begged.

"What did you say to him?"

"Nothing."

"Did you tell him about the cabin?"

"No."

Dale reached down with his other hand and grabbed Niles's neck, squeezing that as well. "Don't fucking lie to me! Did you tell him about the cabin? Did you?"

"No!"

Dale let him go. Niles wanted to vomit. He lay on the cement for a moment before lifting himself up and flopping back into the chair. Pain radiated through his hand, and he massaged it with his other hand.

"Just leave," Niles said. "I don't want you here. I don't want you in my life."

"Oh, but you got me in your life. You're my son, and I'm your father. Nothing will ever change that. Ever." Dale leaned back again, relaxing as he picked up the package of cigars and took one out. "Doesn't matter if you told him about the cabin. I've got a little surprise waiting for him there."

Niles looked over at him. The most horrifying aspect was how alike they looked. Niles could see his eyes and nose in his father, and it revolted him. "What did you do?"

Dale grinned. "You'll just have to wait and see, I guess, won't you, son?"

40

The glass rained over him. Scrapes and cuts stung his arms and cheeks. He felt the shards go down his neck and nick his ear. The sound was so loud it made his ears pound, but he was through.

Stanton landed on the carpet hard. He fell on his elbows and knees and took a second before he opened his eyes. Checking himself, he saw several cuts on his hands and fingers, but it didn't matter. He let them bleed.

He rose and unlocked the front door for Thomas and Katie before pulling out his firearm. Dale would know he was here now. They didn't have much time.

Stanton didn't wait for the others. He ran to the kitchen and then the bedroom, looking underneath the bed. He checked the bathroom and the closets, but no one was there. A set of stairs led down to the basement, and he stood on the top step. He heard Katie whisper his name in the other room and knew what she wanted: they wanted to lead this. This was their jurisdiction and they had to be the ones to find the girl.

No, he thought. *Not for this.*

He ran down the steps, raising his weapon on the bottom step before opening the basement door.

As he hurried into the basement, he froze. His guts tightened so much it felt as though he would vomit. Thomas and Katie came rushing down behind him.

Thomas said, "You can't just—"

"Turn around," Stanton said.

"What?"

"Something's not right. Turn around."

Slowly, Stanton began to back away, pushing the two of them with him.

It was a subtle thing, just a glint of crimson light, but Stanton saw it. It moved across the room, over his shoulder, and moved toward his head.

"Get down!"

The shot shattered the window. A loud, echoing boom in the neighborhood. Another shot, this one tearing away chunks of wooden beam and drywall. Stanton turned, crawling toward the stairs as another shot rang out from somewhere in the darkness outside.

He pulled Katie along and went for Thomas, when he saw the blood cascading out of his shoulder. The round had gone into Thomas's right shoulder and exited through his back. He was groaning in pain as the blood continued to flow.

"No!" Katie screamed, rushing toward him.

"Katie!"

Stanton grabbed her head and pushed it down just as another shot rang out, narrowly missing the back of her head and embedding into the wall. He held her arm and pulled as he crawled up the stairs. When they reached the top, Stanton crouched and crossed the living room. He peered outside, pulling back just a corner of the curtain, but couldn't see anybody. It was too dark out there.

Then he saw the glint again. It was searching the basement. Across the street, the crimson light flashed for a moment behind some trees as it swept over the house.

Stanton rushed out of the side door and sprinted as fast as he could, circling around the house, hoping that whoever was in those trees didn't spot him. The darkness worked to both their advantage.

He got across the street and ducked low on the grass. Now about fifty feet away from Dale's cabin, he began the slow duckwalk back, his eyes constantly scanning the darkness for any movement.

And then he saw him.

A black figure knelt behind some trees, a massive rifle steadied in front of him. The man was speaking into a phone quietly. Stanton came up around and behind. Each step was measured and soft, the trees rustling lightly in the breeze masking any noise he made.

Stanton was nearly on top of the man now. He held up his firearm and said, "Move your hands away from the rifle."

The man froze. He didn't turn around. Slowly, he set the phone down on the grass, and began to stand up.

"That's not what I said. I said to move your hands. You stay flat on your stomach."

Stanton counted ten heartbeats before the man complied and began getting down to his stomach.

And then, in a flash, he was up and ran.

Stanton was after him. The man ran like a track star. In less than a block, he would be out of view. Stanton wouldn't be able to chase him down. He kept sprinting though, waiting for just enough light to be able to see him, steadied his aim, and fired.

The first shot missed, and the second one connected. Even in the relative dark, Stanton saw a little puff of blood explode out of his leg as the man hit the ground, groaning. Stanton ran up to him and pressed the gun to his chin.

"Lemme go, man. Lemme fucking go."

The man wasn't a man at all. He was little more than a boy, maybe seventeen. He lifted the boy and dragged him up onto the grass before sitting on top of him. Years of ingrained procedure and training told Stanton to read him his Miranda rights and call for backup. He did neither of those things.

"Hey, man. Hey… I was tryin' to get paid, man. That's all. It wasn't nothin' personal, man."

"Dale hired you?"

"Yeah, man. Dale."

"Where is he?"

"How the fuck should I know?"

Stanton lifted his weapon and brought the handle down into the boy's nose. It cracked, and blood began to flow within a couple of seconds.

"Fuck you!" the boy shouted, trying to turn to his side and put his hands against his nose.

"Every time you lie to me, I'm going to hurt you."

"I don't know where he is, man. I swear. He paid me to come shoot up this house. He said to shoot anybody that breaks into his house. That some fools were comin' to rob him. That's it, man."

"How'd he pay you?"

"Cash."

"Where'd you pick it up?"

"Some fuckin' condos downtown, man."

Stanton froze. He holstered his weapon. He had been played, and played well. Katie was running up behind him, her gun drawn.

"Call it in," Stanton said, brushing past her to get to the BMW.

She slapped handcuffs on the boy. "I can't let you leave, Jon."

"What?"

"I'm sorry. A detective's been shot. I need you here. And I'm gonna need your gun."

He took a step toward her. "I'm close, Katie. I know where he is. I can't just stop now."

"And what about Thomas? Your obsession with this almost got him killed. Is that just collateral damage? Well, he's not collateral damage to me. I'm sorry, but this has gone too far. It's time to end it."

"End it how? By letting that little girl die, too?"

"Jon, I need your weapon."

He turned around and began walking.

"Jon, don't make me do this."

"Sorry," he said. "You want my gun, you're gonna have to shoot me in the back."

He didn't know Katie and was only guessing as to what she was and wasn't capable of. He wasn't entirely sure she wouldn't shoot him. By the time he checked on Thomas, who was pressing his jacket to the wound to slow the blood, he could hear sirens and took the keys out of his pocket. He ran back out to the BMW. When he drove past her, he saw she was on the phone and running back inside the house.

41

Stanton left the BMW up on the sidewalk and sprinted into the condominium towers. He put on his best smile and asked the guard to see Niles Brown again.

"Tell him I forgot to ask him a couple questions."

The guard informed Niles and Stanton was allowed up. On the elevator, he pulled out his firearm and held it low. Niles was a part of this too, but not like his father. Maybe Niles was as much a victim as Elizabeth had been.

Stanton got to the door and knocked, after pressing his back against the wall and away from the door in case a round came flying through there. Niles came to the door just like he had the other time. Before he could speak, Stanton hit him.

Stanton hit as hard as he could, a right cross on the mouth that sent Niles flying back into the condo. Blood spattered out almost instantly. Stanton lifted his weapon and pointed it at his head.

"What the fuck!" Niles yelled, staring down at the blood on his fingers.

"You're going to tell me what I want to know," he said calmly. "Where is he?"

"I told you. He's at the—"

Stanton fired. The round blew out Niles's knee, and the condo filled with his screams. Stanton pressed his foot against the wound, causing Niles to writhe.

Calmly, Stanton said, "I will do anything to save that little girl. Where… is… he?"

Niles's eyes moved. Subtly, a slight movement to the left, and Stanton heard the footsteps behind him. He ducked as Dale Brown slashed at him with a kitchen knife. Stanton rolled away, coming up with his firearm.

"No!" Niles shouted. He grabbed Stanton's ankles, throwing him off balance and giving Dale time to rush forward.

Dale, though older, hit like a truck. He knocked Stanton back into the wall, the gun flying across the room, Stanton's body collapsing the drywall behind him. Dale grabbed Stanton's shirt and delivered three quick punches in succession with his free hand. On the fourth punch, Stanton moved away, the fist barely missing him and slamming into the wall. Stanton cracked his head into Dale's nose, snapping his head back before he came up with a knee into his groin. Twisting away, Stanton went for his gun.

Niles scrambled on the floor and grabbed the gun, lifting it up and pointing at Stanton.

Dale laughed, wiping away the blood that dribbled down from his nose and over his mouth. He ran his tongue along his top lip as though relishing the taste.

"You're done, Jonny."

Stanton felt the sting in his lips, the loose tooth aching and beckoning his tongue to push on it. He wasn't going to win this way. Slowly, he backed away to the balcony, collapsing into one of the chairs and letting the blood drip down his lips and onto the cement.

Dale looked at his son and said, "You gonna shoot him?" He chuckled to himself, took the gun, and came out to the balcony. He pulled a chair farther away from Stanton and sat down, keeping the gun pointed at him. "I'm sorry it had to come to this. I always liked you, Jon. You were nice to my boys."

Stanton couldn't think of anything to say. He had dreamed of this moment, the moment when he would confront the man who had changed his life by extinguishing his sister's, dreamed about what he would do or say, and now that the moment had come his mind focused only on the pain radiating through his face.

"I loved her," Dale said. "I loved her so much. She was my first, Jon. From the minute I saw her when your family moved in, to those last moments of her life, I loved her."

Stanton spat a glob of blood and phlegm. "How did she die?"

"I didn't want her to die. I wanted her to live, but she kept fighting me. And that son of a bitch Carter couldn't help himself. He started torturing her, real bad stuff. He wasn't a good man. I couldn't very well let her go, so I had to do something." He paused. "It was painless, if that's what you're worried about. As painless as death could be. I wrapped a plastic bag around her head and she suffocated."

Stanton felt as though he might vomit. He swallowed, a torrent of blood going down his throat from the loose tooth at the front of his mouth. It made him sick, but he didn't show it. He just looked up, into Dale's eyes, and at the gun pointed at his chest. "My father was your friend, Dale. This destroyed him. He never recovered. How could you do that to him?"

"Yeah, that wasn't somethin' I wanted to do. Your daddy was an asshole sometimes, but he was my best friend for many years. I guess that's what love does to you. You don't care about who else it hurts."

"That wasn't love. Love is mutual, and my sister was disgusted by you."

"Now you watch your damn mouth. She loved me and I loved her."

"You were her rapist and murderer. She loathed you. Just like that little girl you have now loathes you. Like you would loathe a worm."

Stanton could see the emotion emanating from the man's eyes as he grew more upset. His hand started to tremble.

"Shut your damn mouth!"

"None of them have loved you. Not your wife, not your son, none of the girls. You wanna know why, Dale? Because you're unlovable. You're ugly inside and out, and no one could ever wanna be with you willingly."

"Shut your mouth!"

Dale lifted the weapon. Stanton jumped at him. The gun went off, but Stanton had him. He wrapped his arms around him and leaned back against the balcony railing. Dale writhed, trying to lift the gun, but Stanton had a good close grip and neither one of them could move much.

"Niles!" Dale shouted. "Help, son. Get the gun, shoot him!"

Stanton said, "No, Dale. We die together today."

Stanton hopped up and wrapped both legs around Dale's hips, pulling him back. The weight of both men flung them over the railing. Stanton's world spun: lights then sky, lights then sky. He held tightly to Dale, who was screaming, but Stanton wasn't afraid. He had known it was going to come to this eventually.

The impact against the water felt like hitting a brick wall. The pool exploded, and suddenly Stanton couldn't breathe and was surrounded by darkness. But Dale was, too. He was underneath him, struggling to get to the surface. Stanton wrapped his legs around Dale Brown, and held him there.

Dale clawed at his face, at his arms and his body. The clawing burned Stanton's flesh, but he didn't let go. Not until there was no movement. No thrashing, no clawing… nothing but stillness.

Stanton let him go and floated to the surface, never taking his eyes off the body underneath him that drifted in the dark and then disappeared into deeper waters.

42

Stanton sat in the back of an ambulance, watching the red and blue lights flicker outside. The media had arrived as well, and he saw several news vans outside. Huddled with numerous detectives and paramedics was a young girl they had found in the trunk of a car. Stanton sat up and stepped onto the pavement. He leaned against the ambulance and watched the girl. She was maybe thirteen, maybe younger, brunette with large eyes like Elizabeth. In the dim lights casting shadows, he thought she was Elizabeth and actually took a step forward to go to her. But a police cruiser pulling away illuminated her for a moment, and he saw that it wasn't her.

Katie came to stand next to him. She looked at the gunshot wound on his forearm. The paramedics had insisted he go to the hospital, but he refused. Not until he saw the girl was safe.

"Was it worth it?" Katie said. "Was knowing the truth worth all this?"

Stanton watched as someone hugged the young girl, and they cried, held in each other's embrace.

"Yes," he said. "It was worth it."

EPILOGUE

The sun broke over the horizon as the plane landed on the tarmac. Stanton hadn't been able to sleep on the flight, though he felt as though if his head hit the pillow at home, he could sleep for a thousand years. His arm ached, his face ached, and a migraine was coming, but he'd never felt this good in his adult life. He felt light, and his mind wasn't racing as it usually was. He wasn't thinking about work, about the darkness that was always there just underneath the veneer of society—waiting, always waiting.

All Stanton saw was the ocean and the sunshine, and nothing else mattered.

He retrieved his Jeep from long-term parking and hit the freeway. Without the top, the sun poured in, and it didn't feel as though the last week had even happened. It felt like some dream he'd just woken up from. Or maybe this was the dream, and the fear that he would sleep again and go back to the gray and the dark tightened his guts.

He almost went home, but he remembered.

He got off on the next exit and within twenty minutes was at Good Friends Pet Care. The clerk behind the counter smiled at him and said, "Oh, we have someone who misses you."

Hanny was let out of his pen, and the clerk walked him in on a leash. The dog leapt forward, breaking free from the clerk, and jumped on Stanton. Stanton paid, and the two of them went outside. He put him in the Jeep and regretted not having the crate with him. He petted the dog, who licked his hand.

"I missed you, buddy," Stanton said.

The dog's eyes were pure. Innocent. No hint of malice or sadism. Stanton put his arm around him… and began to weep. The tears flowed easily, and he didn't fight them. He held on to Hanny and let them come.

The dog let him cry, resting his head on Stanton's shoulder. After a few moments, Hanny licked his face, and Stanton wiped the tears away.

"Let's go home, buddy."

Made in the USA
Monee, IL
25 October 2021